PRAISE FOR ANIMAL GLOBE

"This is a complex historical, political-socio-economic narrative, written as a wonderfully readable allegorical story. Mr. Sabella addresses global history and conflict resulting from social status, class, race, and even climate change. It concludes with an especially thoughtful theological, spiritual, Biblical message, holding up its central location—the Meadow of the Olive Tree—as a hopeful place. Written for a wide audience and begging engagement with the narrative, the book is challenging and provocative."

Dr. Peter E. Makari, Executive, Middle East, and Europe Global Ministries of the UCC and Christian Church (Disciples of Christ)

"Many people live only for the moment and are unaware of, or are unwilling to invest time to learn about, global issues. This novel parallels what we see, and hear in the universe, and describes many transformation tales. This book forces your inner mind to reach beyond what you perceive as reality. A masterful piece that leaves you hypostatic!"

Roger Ramsammy Ph.D., President of SUNY 's Hudson Valley Community College, and Board member of World Federation of Colleges and Polytechnic (WFCP). Winner of Education Leader Award from The United Nation's South America.

"Animal Globe presents itself as a short novel set in a fictitious world where animals dominate the scene and act very much as we humans act. As the title suggests, this fictitious world is inspired by Orwell's Animal Farm, and the reader is soon aware that it tracks our human history since World War I. A native of a land that lives in a state of chronic conflict, Sabella understands the tremendous burdens of unresolved conflicts and missed opportunities. He writes with passion and insight, leaving signals along the way that he has more in mind than a historical review. As Animal Globe draws to a close, the reader is faced with provocative observations about the way we humans make the important decisions that impact our human situation. A captivating read for anyone interested in the complex dimensions of global conflicts, their resolution, and ongoing ramifications."

J. Maxwell Miller - Prof. Emeritus
Candler School of Theology, Emory University

ANIMAL GLOBE

A Novel about Purpose, Choices and Consequences

PETER E. SABELLA

First US Edition September 2022

The Library of Congress has catalogued
this book under Control Number: 2022913680

ISBN 979-8-9866581-0-0 (paperback)
ISBN 979-8-9866581-8-6 (paperback)
ISBN 979-8-9866581-4-8 (kindle)

Design of illustrations and maps:
Fadi Hamdan - Jerusalem
Cover Design:
Antranik Emerezian - Jerusalem

Published by Waterfall Books LLC.
www.waterfall-books.com
Email: waterfall-books@outlook.com

In loving memory of my father,
Emile Sabella

To my daughters,
Carlina and Aline

In Gratitude

To Caroline Lucy Smith,

Without your continued support and encouragement, this novel would have never seen the light.

You are my love & my soulmate.

Foreword

You will not be blamed if, already at the very beginning of this novel, you will be reminded of George Orwell's *Animal Farm*. But you will be mistaken if you will treat this novel as an attempt to repeat the basic plot of that dystopian novel or look at it as a cover for the old story. It is neither. While animals play an allegorical role for humanity, it is more or less where that resemblance ends, and you are invited into an equally mysterious and fascinating tale.

The primary motivation for telling the story in the way it is told is the search for humanity in a world plagued with many chapters and instances of inhumanity. The author has guided tours to one of the most troubled and sacred spots on earth, where noble ideas of divinity and peace are constantly shattered by harsh inhumanity perpetrated by callous individuals and powerful institutions.

The allegory of a victimized Penguin community, running away from persecution and seeking a safe haven in a foreign land, does not prevent it from becoming the victimizer of other species. Such is the story of settler colonialism around the globe.

But you have never read a global analytical story in such an allegorical way. It is refreshing to look at this human phenomenon through a tale of animals moving in lands with names that resemble those familiar to us but are different. The impulses of these human animals are not degraded, but the consequences of their actions are evaluated.

For me, it brought back David Hume's famous assertion that human logic is an animal's instinct in many ways. It also reminded me of Judith Butler's tract on the 'grievable and the ungrievable'—which asks whether we grieved when faced with animal suffering and whether we degrade that suffering when we accuse people of behaving like animals. What happens when animals behave like humans is something you will think about when reading the novel!

Animal Globe is not a story looking for a winner, nor the defeat of the oppressed or the rulers. Neither is it a story about revenge, but a story that highlights 'live and let live'—a celebration of the true meaning of coexistence— as an antidote for the human ability to destroy and to seek domination.

Very much in line with many seekers for an end of oppression in many parts of the world, the novel sees international human solidarity as the prime way different animal species, and whoever they represent in real life, can prosper and live a meaningful and peaceful life on this globe.

Ilan Pappe
Historian & Author of *The Modern Middle East*

Author's Note

In the globalization of the twenty-first century, animals live in the convenience of controlled coops, pens, and caves created by themselves for themselves. For some, they are cozy and convenient. For others, they are hard to maintain. Still, for others, they are not what they strive for. Absorbed in keeping, up-keeping, or seeking, many animals cannot see the larger picture of the Globe they live on.

Within animal ranches, animals have also individually and collectively created systems of beliefs that have become the engine behind many choices and decisions made for their lives. Sometimes, animals directly implement those systems. Other times, they entrust others, often elected by them to enact them.

Animals' belief systems, or how they choose to implement them, do not always correlate with other animals' systems. They might even contradict those of others. Often, any attempt to impose opposing systems on the lives of others leads to a collision. As a result, animal life has entangled itself in a life cycle fed by various hurts, whether felt or inflicted. Animal life has also entrapped itself in a system of hierarchies, beliefs, marginalizations, judgments, accusations, condemnations, and stereotyping that lead to actions and counteractions. In due course, animal life is losing to the logic of chaos of its own creation.

Animal Globe is a small contribution towards a better understanding of the cycle of life. It intends to raise awareness that every animal living on the Globe is an inhabitant of his respective ranch and, equally important, an inhabitant of the Globe. The aftermath of global economies is reshaping the order of comprehensive politics.

As inhabitants of the Animal Globe, animals owe it to themselves to be aware of what is happening around them. Animals are contributing, with or without their knowledge, with their decision or indecision, with their action or inaction, to the definition and redefinition of justice, peace, mercy, truth, and love: vital principles for the well-being and security of life on the Animal Globe.

Peter E. Sabella

In the Beginning,

A bird searched for a place to settle. The bird's color was black, as dark as night. With radiant beauty, three feathers crowned his head, red, white, and blue. His elongated tail is in the colors of the rainbow. Shadowing the blackbird, flying behind him, were four large white birds of magnificent beauty. They had long necks and long wingspans. Each one had wings different from the other three, green, red, black, and white. After a while, the blackbird found a location. Very excited to settle, he kept flying vertically downwards. As he faced up, a cloud and a brilliant light appeared above him.

The blackbird uttered the words, "Let it be." At once, a tree emerged. It continued to change, receiving a shape and purpose beyond its control. Its trunk got thicker and knotted, covered by a smooth ash-colored bark. The thickened tree trunk produced three large branches that grew instantly. Around the base, a magnificent round flower bed was formed. The tree's three branches produced multi-branched leaves, shooting upwards and outwards until the tree grew into a perfectly rounded mushroom shape. Soft pale green painted the leaves on the side facing the heavens, while a silvery gray shade painted the trichomes on the leaves underside. The roots carved the soil deeper. They created a network of endless veins that covered the depths of the infinite land they created. The land produced mountains, oceans, seas, rivers, plains, deserts, and heights. On these, many creatures, called animals, the blackbird also created. After creating the skies, and upon the completion of his work, the blackbird rested. He settled in the center of the tree. The four white birds, whom he called 'soulmates,' settled around him in four distinct locations, forming a rectangle between them, keeping the blackbird precisely in the center. He created everything in such a perfect balance of relationship and inter-dependency.

This place he called the Meadow of the Olive Tree.

The Meadow of the Olive Tree

Many animals on the Animal Globe believe that
'The Meadow of the Olive Tree'
inspires
cohesion and harmony among animal species.

Many animals on the Animal Globe believe that
'The Meadow of the Olive Tree'
disrupts
cohesion and harmony among animal species.

*Animal Globe is a story about free will;
every animal has a choice…!?*

Animal Globe
Ocean
Ocean
Ocean
Ocean
Ocean
Newfarm
Newfarm
Eurainia
Redfarm
Asiania
Eastland
Badlands
Olympia
Nigerland
Australinea
N
S
E
W

Concerning the Geography of the Animal Globe and Eurainia

Eurainia is one of the five Farms of the Animal Globe. It is located between two oceans, one that connects it westwards with Newfarm Farm. Another, on its eastern side, connects it with the Farm of Asiana. To the south, the Midlands Sea connects it with the Midlands. Further south stretches the Farm of Olympia. The Farm of Asiana and an ocean link it to the Farm of Australinea.

Ranches of various sizes and shapes divide Eurainia. Within them are mountains and hills of diverse altitudes. Mountains extend within one ranch, establishing a natural border with another. Other mountains stretch out over multiple ranches. Abundant vegetation of colored trees and a carpet of flowers cover its landscape in spring. Their brown rock edges covered partially with a snowy coat provide a dreamlike environment in winter, attracting most animals' notice and establishing the ideal conditions for cold-weather-loving animals.

Eurainia has many rivers stretching out for miles, generous and endless with their supply of water. Their banks are rich with vigorous vegetation. These rivers originate from one ranch and continue their flow through two or more. The ranches' mountains, hills, streams, plains, valleys, and deep ravines have a tremendous beauty that is the theme of many tender stories among animals.

Penfield is a ranch in the center of Eurainia. Northwest of it is the ranch of Greenfield, the southwest are Rhonefield and Alpineforest. To the south are the ranches of Rhinefield and Rofield. Streamforest and Cezia border it to the east. A unique range of mountains connects multiple small ranches of Eurainia's northeastern side with the massive ranch of Redfarm, which is divided into smaller sub-ranches.

Within the Midlands, and in its center, a small and rectangular ranch called Olivia gives direct access to Eurainia from the west through the Midlands Sea. Cedarland borders Olivia from the north, Applefield from the northeast, Philadelphia from the east, and Egofield from the south.

Whether within Eurainia or from the rest of the Animal Globe, no animal from any ranch, except for penguins and birds of the air, is to cross into a neighboring ranch territory without obtaining the Chiefs' authorization. The passage to another ranch is possible through designated guarded gates only with the Chiefs' permission. Chief Bulls, who lead these ranches, each command an army of loyal dogs to watch over their respective ranches and gates. The bigger and the more prosperous ranches have more dogs keeping watch over their gates than the smaller ones. Watchdogs arrest animals attempting to pass through the gates without authorization. After a stern reprimand, they send them back to their ranch of origin. As long as animals try to abide by their respective ranch rules, life continues in relative harmony.

Furainia
Redfarm
Furainian Ranches
Furainian Ranches
Furainian Ranches
Furainian Ranches
Newfarm
Greenfield
Western Terrain
Penfield
Streamforest
Cezia
Alpine forest
Rhinefield
Rhonefield
Rofield
River
River
River
River
Sea
Guquslave
Ottoland
Midlands Sea
Cedarland
Olivia
River
Ocean
N
E
S
W

uslave
Ottoland
Midlands Sea
Cedarland
Applefield
Desertfield
Olivia
River
Philadelphia
River
Egofield
N
W
E
S
Midlands
Temini

Concerning animal species on the Animal Globe

Six animal species live on the Animal Globe; ruminant-grazer mammals, birds of the air, dogs, pigs, horse-breed mammals, and penguins. Almost half of the animals are ruminant-grazing mammals, animals who graze for food. They include cattle, goats, and sheep. Of these, cattle are the most intelligent. The ruling system adopted by ranches prevents any free grazing except for special occasions and specific locations. So, the rulers have developed a unique food mix, called the feed, as the primary food source for all grazers. In Eurainia, the feed comprises a blend of wheat and barley with some honey. In the Midlands, the feed is a mix of wheat and barley. The ruminant species have to work hard in planting, harvesting, and mixing all year long. An average grazer-animal such as a cow, sheep, or goat needs three rations of daily feed. Besides the feed, only cattle, the bulls specifically, have the luxury to add apples to their daily diet.

Ruminant mammals chew the cud, but it is shameful to do that in public. The cattle stopped that natural habit altogether. To them, only working-class animals like goats and sheep chew the cud! Instead, cattle prefer to eat more apples dipped in honey while watching animals working in their fields. Bulls eat twice the average daily portion their bodies need. In no time, they gained significant weight. Together with their cows and calves, they live a luxurious life with little toil or sweat.

The Ruminant animals' specialization and work vary according to geography. Animal Globe's ranches depend on agriculture for food production. Over years of specialization, certain species excelled in specific fieldwork. Because of these skills, animals created nicknames for each species according to their professional work.

In Eurainia, the dominant working species are the goats[1] of different breeds. Five days a week, they work in the fields from sunrise to sunset. Eurainian sheep[2] are few, but some ranches have more than others. Leaders are not enthusiastic about them. According to them, sheep's average intelligence is not suitable for the changing work environment and the rapid development of Eurainia. Despite that opinion, the leaders still allow them to join in the different works on the ranches.

In the Midlands, things are the opposite. Midlands sheep[3] are the dominant working species, not goats. They are not of high intelligence and depend on more intelligent animals to understand things better. They are emotional and are aroused quickly; their emotional outbursts do not last long. They can adjust to newer realities in no time. Goats[4] form a small but still an essential constituent of the Midlands animals.

The Elderly is another species comprising a blend of a few goats and sheep; Elderly Goats and Elderly Sheep. Animals call them Elderly, not because of age but because of knowledge and wisdom they gained over years of dedicated study of the animal existential spiritual realm. Many animals believe they are trustworthy and seek their advice. Animals believe the Elderly have a higher code or service to other animal species because of their attachment to the spiritual realm. The Elderly motto is, "We are to serve the needs and the well-being of animals."

Some animals are very skeptical of the Elderly. The distrust started hundreds of years ago when the Elderly broke their "code of service" and pursued their personal well-being. Since then, the Elderly's key challenge has been to convince animals of their return to a life of service. Leaders continue to offer them their three daily rations of feed.

In recent years, because of the Elderly Goats' breaking of the code of service, a newer group of Elderly Goats developed, a smaller breed known as Wild Goats. These see things in their particular way, focusing on their ultimate dream of being forever free from work. For the time being, they have to earn their food rations as other animals do. But, while at work, they continue telling goats that the Elderly Goats are lying to them and want to keep enslaving them for their work. They spread rumors that a quicker realization of their "free from work" dream can happen only if they convince more and more goats to join their ranks as Wild Goats. They have convinced some goats, and their numbers have multiplied.

There are six types of birds: pigeons, geese, hens, ducks, hawks, and eagles. The animals are fond of pigeons. They rely on them to pass information within the ranches and over the Globe. Like the ruminant mammals, geese, hens, and ducks take part in the land works. Hawks and eagles have sharp eyes, attentiveness, comprehension skills, and prefer ranch work involving their talents. Birds of the air on the Animal Globe eat seeds of wheat and barley.

The Animal Globe has a large family of dogs.[5] They are of multiple, strong, and heavily built breeds. Ranch leaders thought it a waste to throw dogs' strength capabilities into working the land. Instead, because they also excel in following leaders' orders, they are assigned as security patrols and monitors of ranch gates.

Dogs eat biscuits. To maintain a dog's heavy muscle build-up, each dog needs an average of six biscuits a day. To prepare biscuits, animals add water to a grind of wheat, honey, and apple and dry them in the sun for several hours. Biscuit production takes time and involves adding apples that ranch leaders consider a luxury and prefer to keep for themselves. As a result, the dogs have to work hard to get their biscuit rations. To assure more leader control and increase dog allegiance, leaders have often manipulated biscuit rations.

The Animal Globe is also home to horses and donkeys. They have noble characters and have excellent leadership skills. Given that cattle refuse to work the land, the duty of carting and moving the harvest from one location to another rests on their hard work.

Pigs are a hard-working animal species on the Globe. They are rare in the Midlands and prefer to live in Eurainia. The ranch of Penfield has more pigs than the other ranches put together. Pigs are much more intelligent than average animals. They prefer to use their intelligence to improve their living conditions rather than continue living under the mercy and generosity of other animals. In the past, they have tried to undermine Eurainian ranch leadership. Their rebellious attitude caused other animals to see them as chauvinistic. Despite that, they had power and owned extensive Terrains of wheat, barley, and apples, besides vast storehouses of feed and dog biscuits. Mutual distrust and occasional unhealthy competition developed into heated squabbles with other animals.

Another animal species living on the Animal Globe are Penguins. They live in Eurainia because it has the most suitable weather for their skin complexion and feeding and breeding habits. Like the birds of the air, they are exempted from restricted movement between the Eurainian ranches. Animals agree to that exemption because they know that penguin life depends on free land and water access. Eurainian penguins eat krill and squids found only in bodies of water. Each species within the penguin species has different breeding habits that compel the species to migrate from one ranch to another. Ever since penguins lived in Eurainia, Eurainian leaders have always kept their territorial waters open to free penguin movement. Penguins in Eurainia have more opportunities to interact with many animals.

Unlike Eurainia, the Midlands have few penguins. The warm climate there makes it hard for them to live. These penguins, called Chinstraps, have been on the Midlands ranches for centuries. Their skin has evolved and developed heat-resistant skin mechanisms. They hold that their penguin ancestors lived on the ranch of Olivia even before sheep and goats. True, their bodies neither resemble the rest of the animals nor eat the same food, for they eat only fish. Still, they speak the same language and form an integral part of the Midlands and Olivia. They get their fish from fish ponds scattered around the ranches or from the sea. They share work in the fields and live in similar conditions as the rest.

Penguins combined intelligence, tact, resourcefulness, and creativity to have a fruitful relationship with ranch leadership. Penguins show no rivalry to them. They are on such good terms that they cooperate on Eurainian ranches' well-being issues. That made it possible for penguins to own Terrains that they hired out to animals or turned into ponds for their krill, squids, and fish foods. Leaders gave them sensitive jobs, like controlling the storehouses and distributing food rations. Even though penguins enjoyed the leaders' trust and enjoyed privileges, and excelled in their work, most leaders had hidden intentions. When penguins excelled in work, the leaders, as supervisors, took credit for it. When things went wrong, they could distance themselves and put the blame on penguins.

Penguin interaction with animal species has not always been fortunate. Part of their misfortune was, in fact, their fortune. Many animals envied them because of their freedom of movement around Eurainia and their good relationship with the leadership. Animals developed a somewhat polite resentment towards them. It became relatively easy to persuade them that penguins were behind significant mistakes.

Four species make up Penguins: the Emperor, the King, the Chinstrap, and the Humboldt. Emperor penguins are the largest. They have a vigorous nature, thin beaks, and broad, pale, yellow-colored feathers connecting their ear patches and their dark yellow upper breast. King penguins look like Emperors. Their smaller size and their darker orange cheeks make them distinctive. Chinstrap penguins are even smaller and have thick beaks and a black chin strap that runs under their white chins. Humboldt penguins have thick beaks and are small compared to the Emperors. They have a broader white band around their heads. Of the four species, Penguins consider the Chinstraps the most faithful of penguin species to the teachings of Penguism, the rules concerned with penguin view and conduct in life and feeding and breeding practices. The other three species are ambivalent to Penguism; they have forgotten most of its principles and try to lead a life of integration with Eurainian animals.

Concerning behavior and organization on the Animal Globe

Over the years, each animal species gained stature and reputation. The Chiefs of the Globe's animals are cattle. Bulls have earned most ranches' leadership because of size, intelligence, smart looks, and mostly their massive wealth. Animals measure wealth by ownership of acres of wheat and barley Terrains and the quantity of feed stacked in storehouses. Almost all bulls are field owners. Their storehouses are abundant with animal feed and dog biscuits all year long. Occasionally, the more affluent bulls are extra generous allowing other animals to graze freely in their Terrains. On feast days, they even allow two animals to share an apple. Bulls never share honey with any animal, knowing that its sweet taste, eaten directly and not in the feed, can harm the animals' teeth. From their own experience, honey could also make animals drowsy. Drowsiness does not advance efficient work!

Most animals appreciate the bulls' intelligence and are very much dependent on their wealth and generosity. Animals are likewise grateful for the bulls' generous gesture of allowing them to graze freely in their fields on weekends and on two consecutive weeks every spring and summer. As a result, after every four years, when leadership elections have occurred, the bulls have always won the race against the less fortunate goats, sheep, horses, or pigs. Each ranch has its prime Leader, known as the Chief of Chiefs, for four years. Animals can reelect him for future cycles. With the counsel of three others known as Chief Bulls, he oversees his respective ranch affairs.

The progressive way of animal life in Eurainia, together with the tremendous work animals have to do towards sustaining their respective ranches, requires them to exert immense body energy. Chief Bulls help animals produce the needed energy by mixing honey with their feed. Unlike the Midlands, where animals consume honey as a luxury, Eurainian animals consider it a necessity. They need an endless supply of it. But most Eurainian ranches lack enough beehives because of cool temperatures. So, they import it from other ranches, especially from the Midlands that is oversaturated.

Notes about the animal species:

1. Huge ***Valais BlackNeck*** goats have razor-sharp, long, curved horns. During the harvest season, they walk in the middle of tall stalks of wheat or barley fields and swing their heads left and right, chopping them off precisely where they are supposed to be cut, two inches above the ground. ***Valdostana and Tauernsheck*** goats excel in separating the wheat from the chaff. The ***Poitou,*** with their tiny hooves, excel in plowing the land. ***Landrace*** goats can blow the chaff from the grains without much toil.
2. Eurainian sheep are two different species, the Pramenka and the Dales breeds.
3. Midlands sheep are of the **Awassi** and **Arabi** species.
4. Midlands goats are of the Damascene breed.
5. Dog species are the Rottweiler, Boxer, Pitbull, Husky, Bullmastiff, Wolfdog, German Shepherd, and Dobermann.

PART ONE

CHAPTER ONE

Birth: Herman's Dream

One day, on a frosty winter morning, in the delightful Rhinefield Ranch, Herman was sitting in his cubicle, reflecting upon his most recent writings. He was a young, clever penguin born to a well-bred Emperor penguin family. He was thinner and taller than most other Emperors. His chin had developed a unique oversized blubber that was packed densely with plumes resembling a beard. For penguins, blubber was a sign of wisdom.

In his book, Herman wrote,

"It is obvious and beyond any reasonable doubt that, given the last unearthed evidence by bulls of Rhonefield, Curtis the penguin is innocent. In sharp contrast to truth and justice, Chief Bulls tried to hide his innocence, fabricated evidence, and used it against him to keep him incarcerated. I can only think of one reason; it is because Rhonefield hates penguins!"

Herman hardly noticed a pigeon standing on the ledge near his window, calling his name.

"Herman, Herman." The pigeon called and knocked with his beak on the glass window near his stool.

"Herman."

Herman finally noticed him. He sprang up, opened the window, and let him in.

"Oh, I am sorry, my friend, I was writing down my final thoughts in my book and did not notice you," he said with a cautious smile.

"Well, I have sad news for you," said the pigeon. "The ranch owners around Eurainia imposed new rules that confine penguins even more. The pigeons of Eurainia tell me that the number of penguins allowed in school has diminished. In Rofield, there is no more free access for penguins through any sea or ocean. The Chief Bulls there have forced penguins to live in one pond."

Alarmed and disappointed, Herman said, "Oh no, more restrictive measures! It is only a matter of time when the rest of Eurainia will follow, and penguin life will become an endless nightmare!"

Then the pigeon continued, "Penguin free-access privileges to the sea are no more. From now on, the restrictive movement rules will apply to penguins. Only under the watchful eyes of access points and blockades controlled by Eurainian dogs can penguins pass back and forth. Chief Bulls will castigate any penguin caught trying to use alternative access points."

"I cannot say that I am surprised; Rofield's Chief Bulls and Elderly Goats have always blamed us for the death of their Master Fish," said Herman.

"What do you want to do, Herman?"

Saddened by the news the pigeon brought, Herman looked into his book, closed it, and held it next to his heart. The pigeon watched him and thought he saw tears in his eyes when Herman said, "Penguins do not deserve this treatment; we have been treated unjustly for so long. The Eurainian animals are unwilling to let us be who we are; we are a unique species of animals with habitat requirements that differ from theirs. Still, we want what they want: a normal life!"

At this moment, Herman turned away. He looked distant, as if he were in a different world.

Herman cried with a sincere voice, "Is it our mistake that we work harder than the other animals? Is it wrong for us to be wealthier than others and have more fields?" His agonizing tone became even higher. "It is our hard work that made many ranches prosperous, and this is how they repay us!"

Herman was so furious that the pigeon had to yell out,

"Herman, Herman, are you alright? Calm down, my friend."

Coming back to reality, Herman said with a deep tone full of agony and pain, "My friend, no matter what we do, we will always be guilty penguins in their eyes. There is nothing we can change; the past generations of penguin tragedies will continue to haunt our present. We can never assimilate with goats, sheep, and donkeys as long as they hate us."

The pigeon was about to speak when Herman stopped him.

He said, "There is nothing you can say; please take this book. I have put my thoughts together to find a solution to the penguin problems in Eurainia. Take it and make it known among penguin friends. Tell them I want to meet with them soon."

Before Herman tied the book on the pigeon's back, he could read its title: *The Penguin Ranch.*

The pigeon flew with the book to the four corners of Eurainia, and, after time, news of it spread over the penguin world. Many of the Emperor, King, and Humboldt penguins sent the pigeon back to Herman with the message,

"We cannot wait to see you to further discuss the matter."

The Chinstrap penguins, very cynical, asked the pigeon to tell Herman, "What a ridiculous idea!"

A few months later, Herman convened a night meeting in one barn of Alpineforest. Two hundred penguins from seventeen Eurainian ranches attended it. Behind the central podium, two large white flags hung, each with a black penguin's silhouette at its center. As Herman waddled into the barn, penguins approached him with smiles, sharp nods of their heads, and chattering sounds. After the warm welcome, Herman stood in the middle and said,

"Dear penguins,

I salute each one of you for attending this meeting. With

your presence here today, you are taking part in the most historical gathering of penguins ever. Whatever decision we take will be significant to penguins' good on the Animal Globe."

A clamor of nodding and step dancing started.

"Penguin life in Eurainia is becoming unbearable. Every day, ranch owners introduce new rules and regulations that hamper our development and reduce our freedom. In Rofield, Chief Bulls ordered penguins to live in one pond. Daily, they attack our fields and empty our barns of their feed contents without our consent. How can we feed and reproduce under such conditions? Years ago, these were individual incidents, and we reacted little to them. Still, over the last few months, their proportion has increased to alarming levels. As we waddle in the fields among goats, sheep, and donkeys, we hear insults and words of condemnation. "Fish eaters," "long beaks" are examples of what we face daily.

"Fellow penguins, we have strived for total integration. We have adjusted to various unfair rules for a long time. We have failed to integrate, not of our fault, but because Eurainia's animals do not want us. They hate us!"

Another uproar of nodding and step dancing started. A few penguins shouted, "Yes, they hate us! They hate us!"

Herman nodded, waddled to the higher podium, and resumed his talk in a sad and more serious tone.

"I invited you here today, hoping to present a solution to this lifelong struggle we face in Eurainia. Until when do we have to waddle in fear? Until when will animals who hate us for no other reason than our being penguins control our destiny? We owe it to our chicks to guarantee them a safe haven for breeding and feeding."

Herman paused for a moment, looked at the barn from one end to the other as if he were inspecting whether he had everyone's attention.

"After much thought, I can think of one solution; a ranch of our own, a Penguin Ranch where we will be masters of our destiny."

"Ridiculous," yelled a penguin.

"You must be crazy," said another.

Still, others yelled, "What a genius idea," "A great idea."

The idea of a Penguin Ranch split the audience between supporters and opponents. Penguins were yelling at each other and forgot that Herman was giving a speech. They noticed Herman waiting for them to finish their arguing.

When they were silent again, he continued, "I understand that to many penguins and to animals, this idea sounds far-fetched and ridiculous. I tell you what is ridiculous! We cannot go on living under these horrible conditions. The only promise I can guarantee you is more misery and wasted integration efforts in a reality that will keep hating our very existence.

"Fellow penguins, wake up! We must accept the fact ourselves that we differ from every animal on the Globe. We, too, must understand and accept that we have a chance for real freedom. The Penguin Ranch is true freedom from the tyranny and agony of Eurainian animals.

"But I cannot do it alone; I need the penguin spirit. I need your help and devotion. Together, we can make it happen, no matter how long it takes."

"But how can we realize it if penguins live in vast settlements scattered around the ranches of Eurainia?" asked a penguin.

"When we have our ranch, penguins can call it their 'Homeland' or 'Mother Ranch' no matter where they are in Eurainia. They can come to it and start a peaceful life. Instead of emigrating to their usual breeding settlements, they can emigrate to their own mother, Penguin Ranch. They will be safe from dangers and attacks of other animals."

After a compassionate look, "With your help, we will prepare it with conditions for penguin life."

Herman felt his words made a positive impact on his listeners. He moved on to his next point.

"At first, I had a few places in mind where we could realize our ranch. With the help of penguins present here today, I realized," Herman said while looking at two penguins standing at the barn entrance, "that Olivia beyond the sea is the perfect location to create the Penguin Ranch."

A Humboldt penguin interrupted him, "But Olivia is in the Midlands, far away! Our skin complexion will certainly not survive the hot weather there; it hardly rains or snows there!"

Herman replied, "Olivia is full of glorious memories of our forefathers who lived there long ago. Yes, the weather has changed radically. Few penguins live there now, a few of whom have migrated recently. That, my friends, is good news; penguins are living there now! It is thus clear that penguin skin can adapt to any weather. I assure you that this issue will be a minor one since we will bring in expert penguins to find a quick solution!"

"And what about animals who live there?" another penguin asked.

Herman answered him with an unmistakable voice, "Yes, these animals, they call themselves 'Seminoles.' They include sheep, goats, and donkeys. They have always been there, living side by side with our ancestors. Seminoles should not bother us much; first, they are few. Second, all they care about is working their land, harvesting their Olives, tilling the soil, and finding grazing pasture.

"Naturally, we will help them find new homes in the fields of neighboring ranches. Yes, dear penguins, Seminoles should not bother us! Let us concentrate on our destiny. Long ago, our forefathers in Olivia were ambitious and fought prolonged battles against an atrocious enemy, but they have failed. Our enemies walloped us, and we, our own skin, were forced out of Olivia.

"Now, penguins, now, we have a real chance to return to our ancestral homeland and be free. We must seize it!"

Herman's excitement was overwhelming as he said these

words. He started step dancing and turning his head left and right.

"Well, if we entertain the strange idea that Seminoles will accept relocation elsewhere on their own accord, but what about Eurainia's ranch owners? They will prevent us from taking Olivia! And do not forget that they hate us!" said another penguin at the far end.

"Eurainian ranch owners are laying claim to ranches in the Midlands, appointing themselves landlords. If they can do that, so can we, penguins. I am not saying it will be easy. We have to show resilience and courage. To Eurainians, we can be the best illustrators of their progressive habits against the more primitive habits of the Seminoles of Olivia. For that, they will respect and admire us!

"Believe me! Penguins, it will not be long when these penguin haters become our most loyal friends. To look at it from their perspective, they are ridding themselves of the penguin burden!"

Herman's answers were rather appealing, enough to satisfy the curiosity of most of the attending penguins. He divided the attendants into groups of twenty. After a few hours, he deliberated with group leaders and then said,

"Our resolve is done.

"We will adopt the name 'Penguinists' for ourselves.

"Our motto is to establish the Penguin Ranch in Olivia through its redemption.

"We will empower the penguins who have migrated there and help more penguins migrate and redeem the rest.

"Once we redeem Olivia, we will establish our dream Penguin Ranch.

"Before, during, and after establishment, we will stimulate other penguin species on the Animal Globe to love the Penguin Ranch even if they decide not to migrate to it.

"We will likewise encourage other animals sympathetic to our cause to offer to help the organization and create the living conditions for penguin life there."

Herman pointed to the flags behind him and announced,

"Our flag will be a white cloth with a black penguin silhouette in the middle. It will be a symbol of unity for penguins gathered in their new haven homeland."

He wrote under it three words,

"Redemption, Establishment, and Stimulation."

The Penguinist Ranch Flag

"Remember these three words, dear penguins. From now on, these words summarize the rules of Penguinistism. They are our motto and course of action. Never deviate from them, for we are Penguinists!"

The newly born "Penguinists" present started tapping their feet and bobbing their heads with excitement. At once, the whole barn sounded a jumbled chorus of squawking, honking, chattering, and callings of joy. The enthusiastic penguins almost broke their necks from the powerful nodding.

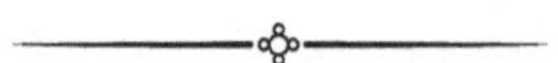

Herman continued working year after year to realize his dream ranch. At first, he put effort into winning one of the penguin species, the Chinstraps. He wanted to win them over since most penguin species appreciated them, irrespective of the fact that besides their similar body features, they shared nothing in common with Penguinist teachings. Penguins considered them the most honorable and truest adherents of the ancestral ways of penguin life. The Chinstraps indeed boasted over that at every chance. They were always trying to enforce their practices on other penguins. Herman, therefore, sent Emperor delegates to leaders of Chinstraps at Streamforest Ranch, which had the most significant number.

"You Penguinists and those penguins who follow you have deviated from the true ancestral ways of Penguism. You forgot our eight principles." said the Old Chinstrap with a growling tone as he recited the principles:

1. One Creator created all animals.
2. All animals he created equal.
3. Penguin practices exemplify the magnificence of the Creator.
4. Penguins eat only fish.
5. Penguins do not kill other animals.
6. Penguins must promote peaceful coexistence among animals.
7. Penguins migrate for breeding.
8. Penguins' life is deeply connected to the Meadow of the Olive Tree in Olivia.

"You tell Herman that his idea contradicts these principles. The idea of a Penguin Ranch is preposterous. We have invested enormous effort over many years towards integration and peaceful coexistence with other animals in Eurainia. Are we just going to drop this idea for a ridiculous dream ranch? A Penguin Ranch contradicts penguin migrating lifestyles.

"Here in Eurainia, we can travel according to our breeding and feeding needs from one ranch to another. A penguin ranch in Olivia removes any possibility to migrate between ranches. How can we even listen to any of your ideas if you, Penguinists, keep feeding on tainted krill and squids instead of fish? How?

Tell me that! What are you thinking?

"This idea of yours will surely lead penguins to more divergence from our principles! We will never agree with you!"

When Herman heard this scolding and uncooperative answer, he felt dismayed. He thought,

"If we do not convince Chinstraps, it will be tough to convince other penguins."

So, he sent his delegates to Penfield and Greenfield, where he encountered rays of hope. His representatives were successful with many Emperors, Kings, and Humboldts who joined Penguinists who migrated to Olivia.

The years passed by, and Herman's health deteriorated. He continued diligently trying to realize his dream ranch, but he could not realize it. Three years after writing his book, he died without seeing many fruits from his hard work.

CHAPTER TWO

THE RISE OF MR. CAESAR

Several years after Herman's death, a global drought, the first of global magnitude, struck many ranches on the Animal Globe. Besides the natural causes of death resulting from excessive heat and lack of feed, many animals died from atrocities committed by other animals who turned very vicious. In the end, surviving animals had to withstand tremendous suffering and hunger.

A year after the beginning of the cruel drought, Lord Marshal, a bull, the Chief of Chiefs of Greenfield, and Mr. Pixner, the Chief of Chiefs of Rhonefield, found out that the ranch of Penfield was behind the drought. Lord Marshal was a brown bull with a big, red head and old, twisted horns. With piercing round eyes, thick eyebrows, and a deep voice that expressed eloquent and carefully chosen words, he commanded and gained the respect of many Eurainian animals. Lord Marshal was astute and wise. He had an individualistic personality and was very reserved, spending a significant part of his time alone reading and writing. The strains of life and heavy responsibility as Chief Bull had him develop the habit of chewing the cud, unlike the other bulls. They refrained from the practice, whether in private or in public. When he talked, he made strange, socially unacceptable pauses.

Eurainian animals ignored Lord Marshal's unusual habits since they knew they resulted from his deep concern for their well-being and relentless effort to resolve their problems. Responsibility had drained his body, and even though it weighed him to a slow but eloquent pace, he always kept his head up in the presence of other animals.

Mr. Pixner was a black bull with a big, round, white head and massive horns. His body was exceptionally tall and dwarfed any animal standing beside him. He, too, was brilliant and had impressive leadership qualities.

Lord Marshal and Mr. Pixner found out that Penfield's Chief Bulls allowed their pigs a deliberate change in their feeding habits. Their investigation uncovered that pigs, unlike other animals, had added a part of corn to their feed rations without the consent of any other ranch. Corn was a new seed brought from the Farm of Australinea. No ranch knew Penfield planted it in large quantities. After mixing it to the feed, when pigs excreted their manure into the soil, it interacted. It created a substance that turned into a poisonous gas that at once killed animals who came in direct contact with it. When the gas reached the upper atmosphere, it disrupted the Globe's protection from the sun's rays, causing the drought.

In retaliation, to protect animals, Mr. Pixner and Lord Marshal imposed harsh punishment on Penfield's animals. They made them work double shifts in the fields to till, plant, and harvest for many Eurainian ranches affected by the drought. They likewise forbade Penfield's Chief Bulls from planting any corn. Penfield tried to explain that many of their pigs had become dependent on corn as part of the feed supply mix and would die. Both Chiefs rejected that claim and insisted that they stop planting corn altogether. Penfield's animals should eat the same feed that the animals in their respective ranches ate.

Penfield's Chief Bulls deliberated for days. They begged the two leaders of Rhonefield and Greenfield for mercy, stating another time that the standard of life in Penfield would drop if they stopped planting corn. The two Chiefs were unwilling to yield. They even hardened their positions. They did not allow Penfield's animals to graze, neither on the weekends nor in the summer times. After two years of such horrendous circumstances, Penfield's animals could barely stand; they were inflamed and deprived of any rest. Above all, they were upset that their hard farming work was being loaded onto carts and taken away to neighboring ranches.

The Animal Globe's drought continued, and its streams were drying out. This affected Eurainian ranches, as well, which were used to having rain and had many rivers. It compelled their animals to live around the surviving smaller rivers that became overcrowded. The cows' udders did not produce enough milk for their calves, the goats for their bucks, and the dogs hardly had any biscuits to eat. Soon enough, various diseases infected many animals, who perished. Others became callous and used many brutal ways to steal the feed rations of weaker animals.

Despite the drought that hit the good and evil, the strong and the weak, Eurainian Chief Bulls showed no mercy towards Penfield's animals. They continued to compel them with the dire duty of work to feed many ranches in Eurainia. Penfield's pigs were more agitated, for not only did they have little to eat, but they also believed that the lack of corn in their feed meant less intelligent pigs. It was not long before they, with the rest of the animals of Penfield, showed complete dismay with their leadership. In the next leadership elections, instead of choosing the usual bull species as Chiefs, they elected unanimously a boar named Caesar as their new Chief of Chiefs.

Caesar was a short boar with deep round eyes and menacing tusks. Unlike other pigs, his nostrils were more extensive than the average pig with densely compacted hair under his nose. There was something about him that puzzled Penfield's pigs' minds. He had the right personality and charisma that the animals needed most. To them, he acted like a pig of his word. Caesar trusted no animal but a few pigs. He immediately and entirely renounced Eurainia's governing system of having Chief Bulls and appointed a small group of pigs he trusted as Chief

Pigs. Together, they rejuvenated hope, but that hope turned into a system of fear and oppressive control as the years progressed.

Like Chiefs of Chiefs in Eurainia, Caesar delivered an opening speech outlining his strategy for the coming years.

He said, "I promise you that the double-work shifts will end soon. I promise that from today you will have the food you need. But I need your full support and cooperation."

Animal life in Penfield was so miserable that they saw a restoring hope in his words and followed him blindly. His remarks were so compelling to the young boars, who promised allegiance. They formed a fighting drift, pledging to follow his orders; he called them the Leaders.

Caesar invested much time watching dogs' behavior. He understood more about the psychology of dogs than any other Chief in Eurainia. He understood pigs had to win their allegiance and obedience. The best way was by worthy rewards. The greater the prize, the higher the allegiance. Likewise, he learned that once a leader wins a dog's trust, he cannot lose it. The dog would obey a Chief's order even if it meant he had to sacrifice his life! The last thing he learned was that hungry dogs were more prone—because of their solid, wide jaws—to do anything to satisfy their hunger than other animals. He thought for days of a way to capitalize on that knowledge.

Finally, he found the way. He ordered his Chief Pigs to keep most of Penfield's puppy dogs in separate fields and barns from the rest of the animals. Leaders were to feed them daily. Each Leader provided the same puppies with biscuits until they matured—this way, they established and strengthened the bond of leadership. The Leaders then trained the mature but young dogs, promising them rewards upon completing their training tasks. They instructed them to jump over fences, crawl under hedges, form ambush circles, and give out menacing growls. After only a few months, Caesar, the Chief Pigs, and their Leaders had a superior obedient dog army.

Caesar still needed to turn his army of dogs into killer

dogs. He and his Chief Pigs loathed penguin species. Caesar blamed them for plotting to overtake Penfield secretly. Other times, he called them "viruses," the prime reason behind every malice befalling Eurainia. Because of such false accusations, coupled with the intrinsic dislike in many animals' upbringing in Eurainia towards penguins, he and the Chief Pigs instructed the Leader Pigs to secretly use penguins as experimental subjects to train the army of dogs. The Leaders released a few detained penguins during training, and the dogs raced to kill them by breaking their necks. The dogs who excelled in killing penguins were rewarded with a biscuit.

A few months later, Caesar summoned the Chief Pigs and announced that his young spy hawk, Vladimir, had found a barn full of feed and biscuits in the neighboring ranch of Cezia.

"What are you waiting for? Feed and biscuits are waiting for you! You must prepare for the attack."

The Chief Pigs prepared attack plans and presented them to the Leaders. They promised high army rankings upon the completion of their tasks. The Leaders prepared the dogs for battle, promising them twenty biscuits upon the mission's success in Cezia.

The awaited battle day arrived. At midnight, Caesar summoned the Chief Pigs at the head of a pack of fighting dogs and a group of fierce Leaders at the main gate leading into Cezia.

He said, "The days of Penfield's misery are finished. Today we prove to the Globe animals that we will not be subdued by their tyranny anymore. You are strong because you follow my strict command and training. I am strong because I have you as my eyes and ears. I have doubled the food rations for each one of you who kills more animals. As proof that I trust in your abilities, I have ordered the attack on Rhinefield ranch as well. I have dispatched another group of my Chief Pigs, Leaders, and loyal dogs to its gate, and they too are ready for a similar attack. When you attack, only think, "kill more, get more.""

The dogs barked in a frenzied passion and attacked the gate. They jumped first at the patrol dogs defending the gate. Outnumbered and less motivated, the defending dogs fought hard to protect the gate, but they could not hold for long. They killed thirteen dogs. The rest fled. With the gate breached, Caesar's vicious drift and pack attacked. At the sight of an animal, a dog jumped and broke his neck. The pigs pierced the bodies of animals with their sharp tusks. They hideously killed many young and old goats, hens, cows, penguins, and bulls. Pigeons, too, were caught by surprise. Two of them tried to fly from a porch, only to find two ferocious dogs on a higher one. The dogs aimed for their necks and broke them. During the attack, the dogs and boars repeated the phrase Caesar taught them, "Kill more, get more." The dogs looked around them; Cezia was under their total control. They were so motivated that they took it in one hour.

Caesar, who followed behind, stepped forward and pointed his trotter towards a green barn.

"This is where they hid the feed and biscuits; your reward is waiting," he said.

Another pig running behind arrived and announced that Rhinefield had fallen under Caesar's control. The dogs opened the door and found precisely what Caesar told them. He gave them their reward of biscuits and feed. He had the surrendering goats, bulls, and horses load the food on carts and take it to the animals in Penfield. In Rhinefield, the pigs found lots of feed. The total quantity was enough to feed Penfield's animals for another six months. Caesar declared the two ranches, Rhinefield and Cezia, were completely subdued. At once, pigeons transmitted the news in Eurainia.

Three days later, Caesar assembled his Chief Pigs for a secret meeting. The meeting was to decide what to do with penguins in ranches Penfield conquered. In conclusion, they used every means to force them out!

Caesar said, "For the time being, keep your actions a

secret." Caesar and his Chiefs ordered the dogs to confiscate the fields of the richer penguins! When asked why, dogs were to answer, "It is your chance to prove your care for the animals of your ranch!" They also prevented them from access to their food ponds of fish, krill, and squids.

When the penguins complained, the Chief Pigs answered,

"Something contaminated these ponds, and we are working on purifying them for you!"

They took the young penguins into secret fields and put them under army watch. The Chief Pigs explained, "The young penguins are doing their duty to their ranch!"

It was in no time when more penguins were leaving Cezia and Rhinefield.

While Eurainian Chief Bulls were deliberating on Penfield's insubordination and assault, the drought ended. It rained day and night for several days. The sight of green shrubs and wildflowers after painful conditions was so satisfying for the animals of Eurainia. Eurainian Chief Bulls invested their time developing quick ingenious ways to feed their hungry and suffering animals. That was more urgent than squandering time on plans to punish Caesar and Penfield. They decided that Penfield's reaction was 'understood as a relief-from-frustration and not a deliberate act of aggression.' They concluded, "the punishment we imposed on Penfield was too harsh. We will surely be able to resolve the issue with Caesar peacefully in a matter of days!"

The Chief Bulls could not have been more mistaken; Caesar had not yet accomplished his deceitful plans. While they were contemplating whether their punishment was too harsh on Penfield, he prepared for another attack. His gluttony for food supplies and ambition to secure absolute power was unanticipated by Eurainian Chief Bulls. Caesar dispatched Vladimir, the young hawk, again to spy on the whereabouts of food supplies and examine the other Eurainian ranches' defense mechanisms.

"There is plenty of food supplies in Streamforest and

Rhonefield," he said, "Their Chief Bulls starve the animals, hiding food from them, those hypocrites!"

Caesar remarked, "Well, too bad for them, but there is no better opportunity than this for us. What can I do with this information? I need action plans. I need a good reason to convince the animals of Penfield to collaborate with me."

After a few days of tireless meetings with his Chief Pigs, they found a solution. They called it the *Induced Drought*. Caesar told his Chief Pigs, "We will plant corn secretly. And next summer, we will harvest it, grind it, and mix it with the rest of the animals' food and cause another drought in Eurainia. It will be worse than the first. But, this time, we will prepare Penfield to face it, and others will not." Together with their Leaders, Chief Pigs forced to hard labor the young penguins they sent to the secret fields, planting more corn before summer. After a while, goats, sheep, hens, and ducks joined the penguins; they sentenced them to cruel work. Then Caesar ordered his army, "Prepare for the attack on Streamforest and Rhonefield." Chief Pigs and their Leaders busied themselves for two days preparing them.

On the day of the attack, Penfield caught Streamforest off guard, and it surrendered. Despite the quick defeat, its Chief Bulls dispatched a pigeon to Mr. Pixner of Rhonefield and Lord Marshal of Greenfield, announcing their ranch's capture. Both Chiefs rallied their dogs for the recapture of Streamforest, but it was too late. Caesar's dogs' grip was too tight to loosen. The two Chiefs of Chiefs found themselves in a worse position than they ever expected since Caesar was already moving his army towards their respective ranches. Penfield's Leader-dog sounder marched in large numbers first towards Rhonefield, snapping at any animal of an opposing nature or species. A fierce battle ensued. Mr. Pixner lost half of his ranch, and many animals died. He sent pigeons to ask Lord Marshal's help. Under the circumstances of haste and frenzied organization, he could not muster his dogs to launch much of an organized offensive against the well-organized packs and sounders of Penfield.

At sunset, many dogs from Streamforest, Rhonefield, and Greenfield found themselves trapped on the shorelines of Rhonefield under the continued menaces and sporadic attacks of Caesar's army. They were exhausted, frail, and did not eat for days. With Penfield's army's advance towards the shoreline, the only escape was by the sea. But the distance to the nearest island was far for any dog to swim, let alone in the miserable conditions they were facing.

"They will not see another sunlight unless we do something!" thought Lord Marshal. "But what can we do? If Eurainia is to have any chance of survival, these dogs are our only counterattack! What can we do to save them?"

After deep thought, he arranged a flotilla of boats commonly used by goats who did not swim. Goats used them to cross between fields separated by bodies of water from one another. After long, menacing nights, the flotilla carried the stranded dogs to safety. When Vladimir saw this strange occurrence, he flew over to Caesar and reported what he saw. Caesar dispatched hundreds of dogs for an attack. But a few remaining dogs from Greenfield prevented their advance towards the flotilla. They fought bravely until their last breath. Despite their death in battle, they safeguarded the passage for the others.

Years after the drought ended, Greenfield placed a group of stones, built in the shape of a Greenfield dog, to honor their courage and sacrifice. Lord Marshal called the operation that saved the dogs the Battle of the Flotilla. He and Mr. Pixner could no more be silent about Caesar's actions.

Lord Marshal told Mr. Pixner, "Unfortunately, my friend, the day we feared has come! We must stop this crazy Caesar. From today, there is no escape; Greenfield and Rhonefield must face Caesar and his treachery in battle."

Mr. Pixner nodded his head in consent.

CHAPTER THREE

ANOTHER DROUGHT: WASTED ANIMAL RESOURCES

With three ranches under his total control, and as time passed, Caesar instructed Vladimir the hawk to write slogans that handed over the Penfield's destiny to his hard work. Vladimir generated slogans:

"We were slaves; Caesar freed us."

"We love you, Caesar."

"No fear with Caesar leading us."

Chiefs wrote them in farmyards, in the fields, and even in pens and stalls. They became the everyday talk of the animals in Penfield. Caesar's achievements further increased the pigs' admiration for his leadership. To show that, they called him Mr. Caesar and saluted him by raising their right trotter while saying, "Hey Mr. Caesar." Mr. Caesar fulfilled his electoral promises. He delivered the food Penfield needed desperately and canceled the double-shift work. After a while, the Chief Pigs imposed this salute on Penfield's animals. Most of them welcomed it and expressed it enthusiastically. The Chief Pigs likewise forced the greeting on animals of other ranches Penfield subdued and ruled. Many animals refused to utter it. The Chief Pigs regarded them as "enemies of the establishment." They subjected them to continued surveillance and disciplinary action and sometimes even punished them by death.

On one warm summer day, Mr. Caesar was parading in the

center of Penfield. He was trotting in the middle of twelve dogs, six on each side. A passel of pigs stood in three rows on each side facing him. Behind them were many rows of his disciplined, fierce-looking dog packs and then many animals from Penfield. He received a warm welcome. When he approached the ranch center, a Chief Pig uttered a signal shriek, and the animals lifted their right trotter and said,

"Hey, Mr. Caesar."

Mr. Caesar, pleased with this welcome, raised his right trotter back over and over as he paraded. His firm-looking tusks hid an arrogant smile behind them. A goat, spying for his Chief Pigs, saw two goats not raising their right hooves. He reported it to a Leader instantly, and three dogs took the insubordinate goats behind a barn. The menacing dogs encircled them.

"The punishment of insubordination is death!" said one of them.

Just then, the skies dimmed, and two gorgeous white birds penetrated the clouds over Penfield. They differed from any of the birds of the air the animals knew. To the animals present at the parade, their appearance looked magical. They caught everybody's attention. Everybody was touched. It was as if the two white birds enchanted those witnessing their appearance, carrying them to a different realm of nature and creation. As they flew in circles over the ongoing procession, Mr. Caesar's dogs secured their Chief by narrowing the protective circle surrounding him. The two white birds glided lower and lower. The rest of the animals watched. As they approached, everybody noticed their outstanding elegance, but nobody could describe it. They had massive wingspans. The lower side was extremely white, but the upper side had a different color. They had long tails, and their feathers were so white, capable of reflecting the sunshine. The two birds uttered a profound sobbing sound that was heard everywhere.

As they approached, it looked as though they were heading straight for Mr. Caesar. The dogs tightened their protective hold over their Leader, almost squashing him. When the birds flew over them, everybody noticed their grim looks. They shed red and black feathers mixed with sorrowful tears. Mr. Caesar and his dogs looked up but seemed unmoved by the occurrence. As Mr. Caesar and his entourage shook the wet feathers off their bodies, the birds shifted their attention to the barn where the three dogs held the two insubordinate goats. They shed more feathers mixed with shrieks of pain over them as they flew away. Here, too, the dogs were unfettered. One of them snapped the neck of one of the two goats. The other goat, terrified, bent on his front hoofs and begged for his life,

"Hey, Mr. Caesar; please! Hey, Mr. Caesar; have mercy!"

But the dogs had none.

"Our orders are to have no mercy for insubordination! Goodbye."

As the second dog aimed for the goat's neck, the third dog named Samuel, the youngest, jumped in between them. The two white birds put him in a trance.

"Wait, am I the only one here who saw what just happened? Didn't you see those strange-looking birds crying? I have never seen them before! Wait, don't you sense they are trying to tell us something? Maybe we should give this goat a chance. Look at him; he will never be insubordinate again!"

The two other dogs growled threateningly at him. Samuel fell back with hesitation. At once, the second dog sprung at the goat and cracked his neck. The two vicious dogs turned their attention to Samuel.

One of them said with an intimidating growl, "As a brother dog, consider this your first and last warning. Never question your orders. Otherwise, you will have a similar end. Is that clear? As a punishment, dig their grave alone, and remember, if you behave like this ever again, you will be digging your own hole!"

Samuel, daunted by their threat and under their watchful eyes, dug a hole in the ground and pulled the two goats to their burial place. What Samuel just did troubled and saddened his heart. He thought, "Who am I? What am I doing? And who are these strange-looking birds?"

A King penguin and a young boar watching from the window of the penguin's cubicle nearby saw what happened. Alarmed and terrified, the penguin waddled to the main barn, where many animals were assembled and announced what he had seen.

"Ridiculous, this can't be true; Mr. Caesar loves us," said a donkey.

"We were slaves; Mr. Caesar freed us," said a duck.

The young boar ran towards his father, named Oscar, and described to him what he had seen. Oscar, a wealthy and righteous pig who owned many feed storehouses, instructed his son to be silent until he investigated the matter further. At midnight, the alarmed King penguin took his partner and chicks and three goat friends, along with a donkey, and escaped to Rhonefield. Rhonefield was not under Mr. Caesar's control. A week later, the penguin's family joined dozens of other penguin families migrating by the sea to a ranch called Olivia in the Midlands. They joined a particular group of penguins called the Penguinists.

The dogs killed the goats in haste; they didn't see any other witnesses. The affectionate pygmy goat, Irene, worked in the barn outside which Mr. Caesar's dogs killed the goats. A coat of light brown hair covered her tiny body. She had an exceptionally round white belly. Her forehead had a cross-shaped white fuzz, right in between her short and somewhat-bent-outward horns. Earlier in her life, she had dedicated herself to helping other animals, rather than focusing on goats' natural breeding needs. She was about to start work on a game project for Penfield's little animals. Upon hearing the ongoing heated conversation outside, she pondered whether she should step out and interfere. The discussion's tone was dreadful enough that she dared not even stick her head outside the barn. She kept silent. She could hear every word. As the dogs left the site, she ran outside and shed bitter tears on the two goats' graves. The incident weighed on her heart and deprived her of sleep for many nights.

Over the next few days, and during Mr. Caesar's battles for the takeover of more ranches, animals saw the agonizing two white birds repeatedly in different parts of Eurainia. Their shrieks and cries intensified. Mr. Caesar's hostility towards many Eurainian ranches devastated the well-being of animals. Still, no animal species was more affected than the penguins.

Penguins received much of Mr. Caesar's hatred, deceit, cruelty, and hideous crimes. He always reviled them. He surrounded himself with pigs that hated them as well. In the beginning, his actions were more benign. He only wanted to oust them from Penfield. For that, he supported their migration efforts over the sea to the ranch of Olivia. Thousands left this way and joined the Penguinists. While planning his schemes to attack Eurainian ranches, he killed hundreds of them as experimental subjects to train his army of dogs. He later imposed many cruel experiments on them, trying to find solutions to diseases that befell Penfield's animals during the drought. As his greed for power and more ranches increased, he needed a trained army. He refined and perfected the brutal training of his dogs. He called it "chase, trace, and kill." In it, Leader Pigs released prisoner penguins and allowed them an hour's space to hide. The loyal dogs were then to pursue, find, and kill them. They rewarded the dogs generously with biscuits for their agility and cruelty.

Summer arrived, and it was time to harvest Mr. Caesar's secret cornfields. The Chief Pigs found nifty ways to gather it by putting to work many animals they enslaved from the ranches that came under their control. Starved horses, goats, hens, and particularly penguins labored day and night to gather the crops. Emperor and King penguins twisted the corn ears off the stalk with their long, thin, but by then dull and fatigued beaks. Weary goats then opened their jaws and collected them. With every ear a goat gathered on a cart, a painful scream begging for mercy was uttered. Worn-out horses mustered the power that remained in their withered bodies to pull carts to large barns. Faint goats took one ear of corn at a time between their teeth and pulled back the husks to the bottom. Then the young hens, overburdened with strict time schedules, picked the individual kernels and deposited them into horse-drawn carts, which pulled them to the base of a nearby hill. This happened under the watchful eyes of Mr. Caesar's dogs and Leader pigs. Any animal found attempting to eat even one kernel found his neck snatched by the jaws of a ferocious dog.

Penguins then tied ropes around round-shaped stones that hungry, skinny horses pulled up the hill and then allowed to roll on the stacks of kernels at the hill's base. The horses repeated the arduous and lengthy process until they turned the corn into very tiny pieces. The hens then collected those in carts that the horses painstakingly pulled to barns. They were secretly mixed with feed by pigs loyal to the Chief Pigs. Sometimes, the horses were so exhausted that they lost their grip on a stone. The stone rolled and crushed the penguins and hens in its way. Expert geese, recruited by the Chief Pigs, collaborated with Penfield, supervised this entire process in the barn, and concluded that the mix was perfect. It was impossible to discover any visible traces of the corn inside it. The Chiefs took the feed to the ranches under Penfield's control and distributed it to animals as feed rations.

A few days later, Mr. Caesar's premeditated Induced Drought began. The excretion of infected animals, upon touching the soil, formed the poisonous gas that disrupted the Globe's atmosphere from insulating the Globe from the heat of the sun. Temperatures rose drastically, and rivers dried up. Planting seeds became a nightmare. Mr. Caesar held endless meetings preparing plans for a more vicious attack on Streamforest, Rhonefield, Greenfield, and smaller ranches in Redfield's vast lands. During the sessions, the two magnificent white birds continued to appear in the skies of Eurainia. A third white bird of similar mystic nature often joined them.

When they first appeared, they flew in circles and in an organized manner, as if they were in chorus. But soon enough, their flying pattern changed entirely, looking reckless and disoriented. They flew high up and then took a deep free-fall plunge, and just before hitting the ground, they resumed control and flew straight over the animals' heads. Each of the white birds left behind a trail of feathers in the color of its particular wings, black, red, or green.

Their shrieks became even more intense. They caused no harm to any animal, but their cries were so excruciated that they became the talk of many animals. To Eurainian Chief Bulls and Penfield's Chief Pigs, the white birds distracted the animals from fieldwork and battle preparation. They decided simultaneously but with no prior coordination to hunt them. Enormous dogs waited on barn tops and in open fields, hoping to ambush them. With every failed attempt, the white birds gained more impetus, and their flight patterns became even more disorganized.

In the meantime, Mr. Caesar instructed his Chief Pigs to order his dogs to kill the remaining pigeons in Penfield.

"For this next phase, we have to be careful to only engage the Chief Pigs in planning. We do not want plans leaking out. We must destroy pigeons of our ranch; we only need one hawk, Vladimir. He is very devoted to us. Not only will he spread loyally the messages I want, but he will watch any insubordinate animal."

The rest of Penfield's pigs busied themselves in self-training and training dogs to become more ferocious than ever before. At first, Leaders taught the dogs how to attack by pairs. After mastering that, the Leaders prepared them to strike by fours, then by sixes, and then by dozens. During the training, pigs used more and more penguins to chase, trace, and kill. Finally, the army was ready for serious battles. Penfield's dogs manifested high discipline and blood thirst. On the last day of training, while the dogs slept, Chief Pigs painted on their barns' walls and pens a slogan for them to follow. It read, "Catch an enemy animal, Mr. Caesar feeds you an extra ration. Kill an enemy animal, Mr. Caesar feeds you two extra rations." For pigs, the slogan was easy to learn; they were growing more intelligent, mainly after being able to remix corn to their feed. A few dogs were too excited to remember and could not learn it. Chief Dogs narrowed it to "Mr. Caesar always feeds us."

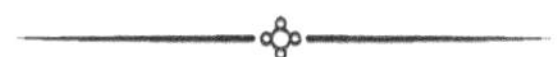

Winter came, but with little rain. The Chief Pigs continued feeding animals with Mr. Caesar's deceitful and drought-causing rations of food. The Globe's atmosphere lost more of its protective capabilities from the rays of the sun. Many animals died. But Penfield had enough feed to last for many months stacked in secret barns. As for water, Mr. Caesar had a flow of underground sources of which only a few select pigs knew the location. They brought the water in enormous barrels pulled on carts by horses as needed.

Mr. Caesar signaled the attack on Rhonefield. In their twelve, six, and four packs, the army broke the necks of and slaughtered many animals.

"Mr. Caesar always feeds us," they kept barking.

They killed more animals than they captured. A few pigeons escaped and flew over to nearby ranches to report the mass murders. Lord Marshal and Mr. Pixner, determined not to let Mr. Caesar get away with it this time, sent their dogs to attack Penfield. Upon their arrival to the battleground, their dogs fought hard. They repelled Mr. Caesar's army, but they got hungry and thirsty after a short while. The battle continued for days. Neighboring smaller ranches to Rhonefield fell to Mr. Caesar's army. Eurainia's fighting army of dogs found it hard to repel Mr. Caesar's dog packs but kept their ranks intact and slowed his advance towards the larger ranches. Fights at the gates intensified. Mr. Caesar's dogs stormed the gates, only to lose them again to the defending dogs. The cycle continued over the battlefields.

Another summer passed; Mr. Caesar's deadly Induced Drought continued ruthlessly, claiming the lives of many animals. The devastation it caused and the vicious behavior of hungry animals that accompanied it had spread to the Animal Globe's diverse regions. Mr. Caesar's disciplined and well-prepared army continued pushing forward, attacking more Eurainian ranches and subduing them. The same contaminated corn mix that continued to poison the atmosphere also fed these ranches. Mr. Caesar and his Chiefs took pride in marching and parading in the fields of the defeated ranches whose animals they reduced to Penfield's servitude. The Animal Globe had never seen such extreme levels of poverty and hunger.

With many ranches under his control, the cunning Mr. Caesar assembled Penfield's animals, without its penguins, in a large open field. After his parade, he found the high podium prepared for him. With his Chief Pigs lined up behind him, he was about to deliver a speech when the skies grew gloomy and the three magnificent white birds reappeared. They flew over, uttering their agonizing screams.

With total disregard to them, he declared with a louder voice, "After investigation, I found the true cause of Penfield's and Eurainia's mischiefs. It is the penguins! Penguins have been surreptitiously interfering in our safety and well-being. They play innocence, but they are not. Animals, our faithful dogs, captured one hundred penguins last week, poisoning our food. Our dogs found penguins mixing corn with the feed since winter!

"That, dear animals, is treason; you know well it is forbidden to mix the corn with feed!" A loud commotion of, "Hey Caesar!" went on for a few minutes. When it died down, Mr. Caesar continued, "And this is not the only thing they did. My loyal

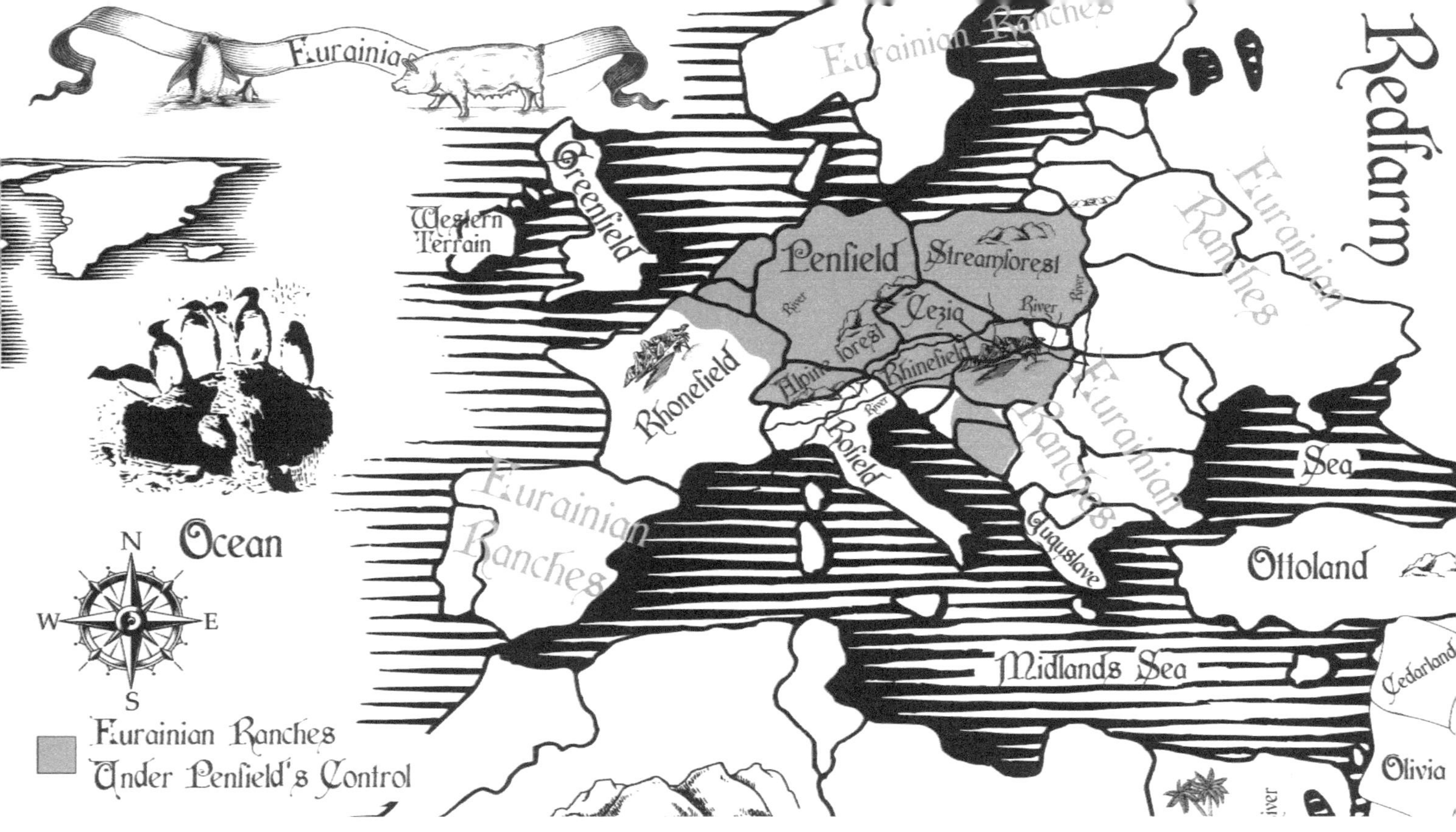

Redfarm
Eurainia
Eurainian Ranches
Eurainian Ranches
Eurainian Ranches
Eurainian Ranches
Greenfield
Western Terrain
Penfield
Streamforest
Cezia
Alpine Forest
Rhinefield
Rhonefield
River
River
River
Rofield
River
Quaquslave
Sea
Ottoland
Cedarland
Olivia
River
Midlands Sea
Ocean
N
E
S
W
Eurainian Ranches
Under Penfield's Control

geese have discovered the real reason behind the drought." The animals present looked at each other with anticipation.

Mr. Caesar called Jorgen, an old goose. He spent most of his adult life traveling and studying animal habitat and life conduct. Jorgen quacked for half an hour.

The animals understood nothing from what he said. They could glean from his quacking three words: penguin, skin, and poison.

Mr. Caesar then resumed his talk, saying, "You have heard it; the corn mixed with feed has had only a partial effect on the atmosphere. Jorgen's investigation revealed that a pig's white skin is the most environmentally safe. Other animal skin types, except for those of penguins, have various degrees of safety. The real reason for the drought was the penguins' black skin, which secretes a poisonous substance that kills animals. You, goats, how many kids have you lost? You, pigs, ducks, hens, and sheep, how many little ones have you lost because of that deadly excretion? We have suffered enough from penguin treachery and duplicity. They knew it but never told other animals. I, therefore, demand an immediate solution to the penguin problem in Eurainia by its total elimination. From today, those parasites have no place in our lives. They cannot live among us or even work in our fields."

As Mr. Caesar got older to a fully-fledged round pig, he mastered the art of controlling his voice with different high and low tones. There was a tone to inspire and another to threaten. There was a tone to remove fear and another one to induce fear. Mr. Caesar had developed body movement skills that charmed most animals listening to his speeches. He had a way of moving his head, combined with skilled manipulation of his eyebrows and control over moving the dense hair under his nose. Mr. Caesar integrated into his speech a whisk of his tail. When he talked, he captivated and bewildered the animals present. Even though the news the animals heard was hard to believe, he swayed their opinion and caused an alarm. In fact, they were so relieved now that they knew the reason behind the drought!

They yelled out, "Hey Mr. Caesar, Hey Mr. Caesar, away with the penguins." Vladimir flew everywhere, inciting animals against penguins.

Penguin life on ranches under Mr. Caesar's control became a nightmare. Many fled to remote ranches. More migrated to Olivia. Yet others refused to leave.

"Eurainia is our homeland," they said.

Many animals were terrified and disgusted at the sight of a penguin. They pushed and pulled them, saying to them,

"You ruined our Globe!"

"You caused the drought!"

"Long poisonous beaks!"

Goats, bulls, and even donkeys cooperated with pigs and dogs to capture and kill penguins. It was hard to tell whether they were cooperating because of fear or want.

Mr. Caesar's dogs trapped and caught many penguins trying to escape to nearby ranches. The Leaders sent them to the secret eastern fields belonging to the pigs. They worked with many enslaved animal species day and night, tilling, planting, harvesting, crushing, and mixing wheat, barley, honey, and corn. Barely fed, they died of starvation. The pigeons of Eurainia disseminated the news of the cruel conditions of penguin life in Eurainia. They said that penguins were disappearing. Vladimir, Mr. Caesar's docile hawk, flew in Eurainia. He explained the penguin disappearance, "The pigs are trying to find a solution to the penguin skin problem and end the atmosphere problems. The Chief Pigs are doing their best to treat the penguins' skin problem!"

He convinced many animals.

In the ranches under Mr. Caesar's control, Vladimir developed a new slogan, "Mr. Caesar is curing the Globe." He flew over animal group assemblies, repeating the motto. Many animals were over-saturated from hearing it; they did not object at the sight of any penguin taken away.

"Mr. Caesar works hard; he is healing the Globe," they said.

The Elderly Goats, the Elderly Sheep, and Chief Bulls called the prevailing violent situation "the Global WAR." They explained that WAR was an acronym of the words WASTED ANIMAL RESOURCES.

This was explained to mean, "Animals must wise up and look at the global picture. They have to see the devastation animals have caused to animal life and resources because of their bigotry, narrow-mindedness, and greed. The loss of animal life and the damage to mother nature could have been prevented if ranch Chiefs got past their egos and talked with sincerity and compassion about the burdens of others."

They could see a fuller picture of the preceding events that led to the unprecedented violent escalation. They gave the earlier drought and its associated violence the same name. To differentiate between them, they gave them numbers: one and two, Global WAR I and Global WAR II, respectively.

Ranches on the Animal Globe found themselves compelled to take sides with Mr. Caesar or his opponents. The Animal Globe's fate was so entwined that any ranch's well-being depended on that of others. Rofield sympathized with Penfield, for their Chiefs of Chiefs shared similar worldviews, absolute rule. In both ranches, the Chief of Chiefs stopped leadership elections that were held every four years. The prevailing conditions required their strong leadership, and animals had to rally around them with full support. Rofield played it safe and tried to act as if it were interested in promoting peace between the sides.

More than once, Greenfield sent pigeons to Newfarm, a massive ranch at the other end of the sea, for help. Its Chief of Chiefs refused to get involved since the drought did not hit his ranch. Newfarm also refused to allow any fleeing penguins from Eurainia access to their shorelines. The penguin water free-movement rule did not apply to Newfarm, resulting in the stranding of many penguins. Newfarm's Chief of Chiefs changed his mind when Japaland, one ranch in Asiana and ally to Penfield for a mysterious reason, attacked a flotilla of Newfarm's army of dogs. Newfarm joined the fight on the side of Rhonefield, Greenfield, and Redfield, tilting the balance in their favor. They were known as the Partners.

Japaland, greedy for more power and ranch control, was previously involved in another territorial conflict with its neighbor Eastland. Eastland, therefore, became an ally of the Partners.

CHAPTER FOUR

MR. CAESAR'S PENGUIN FIRE-KNACKERS

Mr. Caesar's pompous slogans and appearances enchanted many animals. Yet not all! Irene the goat, Oscar the pig, and Samuel the army dog could not accept Mr. Caesar and his Chief Pigs' deceit. All three saw their hypocrisy and cruelty firsthand. They found it very hard to believe that Penguins' black skin caused the drought! But they also knew that they could not announce the truth publicly. They feared for their lives from Vladimir and Mr. Caesar's loyal army. They were always watching for any sign of insubordination and defiance. Indeed, after being direct witnesses to the tragedy of the two goats, hearing pigeon accounts about the Chief Pigs' atrocities to animals in neighboring ranches, and seeing the disappearance of many of their penguin friends, they were determined to help penguins escape death.

They succeeded in various degrees, but not without significant risk to their lives. They had to use their wit, resourcefulness, and utmost vigilance to develop the most innovative ways to save penguins. It took much dedication and persistence.

Samuel, the dog, did not waste time. Being part of the tragedy of the two goats weighed on his heart.

"It is true, I am a fighter dog, but I am not a murderer. I have to do something!"

He resolved not to kill another animal without a just cause.

But, to preserve his own life, he did not want his Chief Dogs to detect his insubordination. He only pretended to implement their cruel orders when he executed them, but he actually did not. On one occasion, at the daily execution place that Chief Pigs prepared for penguins, a Chief Dog ordered Samuel to kill a penguin. Samuel pretended to be abusing the penguin by pushing him back and forth and laughing out loud while insulting him.

"Are you amused, long beak? I absolutely am amused. Come on. How do you prefer to die? Leaning forward or backward?"

When the Chief Dog was not watching him, he sought the opportunity and pushed the penguin further down the hill, whispering the way to escape in his ear. He then barked victoriously, "Hey, Mr. Caesar," assuring the Chief Dog he had executed his order.

The Chief Dog was unaware that Samuel, who knew the place well, had dug a secret tunnel to an underground stream. Samuel found it beside the execution place by accident. He never reported it to his Chiefs. At every free opportunity, Samuel dug the tunnel until it reached the water source. He toiled many nights, missing meals until the tunnel was long enough to get to the stream. He dug the tunnel in a V shape, first going deep in the soil until it found the water that filled it from the other direction. This way, Samuel made sure the stream of water would never rise to ground level and be discovered. When penguins reached the water, they only had to swim up the stream towards safety. Samuel did this often and saved dozens of penguins' lives until his Chief dogs discovered him one night. A dozen dogs surrounded him, and a fight ensued. Their cruel jaws killed him instantly.

Oscar, the pig, owned ten feed storehouses. He was on excellent terms with other pigs since he himself was a pig and provided them with feed. To save penguins, his plan was simple, to use them. He hired them, claiming that he needed more of them to toil in his storehouses, sifting the chaff from the grains of wheat. He said to the Chief Pig in charge, "Send me the penguins you can. I cannot keep up with the supplies you expect without them."

On another occasion, he insisted, "The more penguins you send to my storehouses, the more effective and prompt my supplies will be to you!"

Over the years of the drought, the visits of that Chief Pig increased considerably. He claimed he was inspecting the storehouses' safety, whereas, in reality, he wanted to arrest the penguins Oscar employed. Oscar bribed him with large amounts of feed. Soon, the feed supply depleted. Oscar had to sell his storehouses, one after the other, risking his own children's feed rations to continue bribing that Chief Pig. He never gave up his penguins! By the time the drought ended, Oscar had saved hundreds of them. He died many years later of pig disease.

As for Irene the pygmy, with the aid of a dozen animals, two goats, three hens, one pigeon, one horse, one cow, one duck, two dogs, and one donkey, she organized the safe escape of hundreds of penguin chicks from one of the restricted ponds of Streamforest. Her size and innocent looks made it easier for the pigs to trust her. They gave her the job of finding cures for the various diseases that befell Streamforest animals because of the drought. She had access to the concentrated areas of sick penguins that Chief Pigs used as test subjects. The watchful dogs got accustomed to her presence with the horse that helped her pull the sick animals' cart. Often, she hid penguin eggs or chicks on those carts covered by the ill or the dead bodies. Watchdogs inspected everything coming out of the gate. As dogs approached to sniff the cartload full of sick or dead penguins, she said, "Contagious, my friends; stay away!"

At the word "contagious," the alarmed dogs moved back and let her cart pass.

She did this as often as possible and smuggled hundreds of eggs and chicks to safety. Gigantic hens and ducks then adopted the eggs and sat on them until they hatched. Both birds learned to stretch their bodies so that the hens could sit on two eggs and the ducks on three. One time the duck had to sit on four eggs for two weeks. Irene hid the Penguin chicks behind stacks of large wood in the barn shared by three goats and an old cow until they reached swimming age. A pigeon kept a close watch for any dog patrols. A dog who won an award the year before for his talent in catching fish plunged into a fishpond owned by a Chief Pig and stole fish to feed the chicks. Night after night, Irene and her friends put the grown chicks on a cart pulled by a meager donkey, escorted by another dog. They smuggled them to a distant river and from the river into the sea. Irene and her friends continued their efforts until the end of the second drought and WAR II. She died of natural causes a few years later.

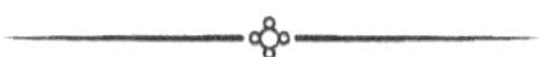

Ever since Newfarm joined the Global WAR, the Chief of Chiefs tried to find a way to end the drought with the least animal casualties. He used a secret remedy developed by one of Newfarm's most prominent geese. The treatment was to add wild gold honey, which was found in rare and remote locations on the Animal Globe, to the mix of feed the animals consumed. After consumption and excretion into the soil, the reaction produced gases that could cause different rain levels. The quantity of wild gold honey added was the crucial ingredient: the more added, the stronger the storm. Until then, Newfarm used it within its vast boundaries to induce regular rain for agricultural purposes. Now, Newfarm intended to use its secret weather control weapon to punish Japaland for its unprovoked attack on its dogs' flotilla days earlier.

As Newfarm's Chief Bulls gave their orders to the army to prepare for a severe storm on Japaland, two wonderful shining white birds appeared in the skies of Newfarm. They flew in circles. Together with their agonizing shrieks and heavy sobbing, they left a trail of white and black feathers mixed with tears. Even though the Chief Bulls and their Chief Dogs noticed them, they remained resolute and did not give their presentation any real consideration. They continued with their plans and preparations.

Newfarm's Chief of Chiefs assigned secret special dog-horse missions to infiltrate Japaland at night. They added the quantity of wild-gold honey needed for a massive hailstorm to the animal feed in two storehouses. After a few hours of consuming the meal, gigantic hail balls as big as a pig's head fell with no warning over vast areas of Japaland. It was the most brutal pounding of hail, accompanied by threatening thunder and non-stop lightning, any animal had ever seen. Animals ran in every direction, trying to find shelter. Any hail ball hitting an animal killed him. Old barn roofs could not withstand the pounding and collapsed on the animals under them. Five goats in one barn and two horses in an adjacent one, escaping from the collapsing roofs, frantically ran out. They were caught by an immense lightning bolt that killed them.

The storm continued for a month. Food supplies ran out, and many animals died of starvation. Vladimir, witnessing from afar the death and devastation of the ranch, rushed to inform Mr. Caesar. On his way, he flew over Greenfield, where a meeting was taking place between a group of geese and enemy Chief Bulls.

A goose, spotting him, said with a loud threatening quack,

"Tell your Mr. Caesar, tell him that his defeat is imminent. If Penfield does not surrender within one week, the same thing will happen to it. The fate of its animals rests on him!"

Alarmed, Vladimir flew hastily to tell Mr. Caesar.

Mr. Caesar, with a beaten and defeated spirit, yet as shrewd and cunning as he was, assembled his Chief Pigs in a secret underground barn on the east side of Penfield. Twelve of his most ferocious and loyal dogs protected the barn entrance.

He said to them, "Years ago, the animals of Penfield lived under the worst conditions an animal could live. Eurainian ranches were unfair to us, pulling and pushing us. They controlled our destiny, stole our food, and forced on us the tremendous burden of feeding thousands of animals in Eurainia. I promised to abolish those double-work shifts, and I fulfilled my promise. We have worked harder ever since, but at least we worked for ourselves and for our ranch out of strength and not of weakness and cowardliness. Look at us now: we control many ranches, and the animals of Eurainia fear us! We have achieved the impossible.

"There is no doubt in my mind that penguins stirred Penfield's destruction. Despite our efforts to get rid of them, they still spread in Eurainia, spreading their venom with their very presence, with their dark skin. They are a danger to animals. It is time for them to *permanently* disappear from our lives. The final solution plans in the eastern fields must start at once. It is the right thing to do! This is my last order to you.

"It is time for me to resign and for our dear Penfield to surrender. But you know I cannot give that order, and they cannot see me weak in front of other ranch leaders. I must go now..."

Mr. Caesar walked out of that barn. His body shrunk to half its size. Six of his dogs escorted him as he climbed a high mountain. He looked at them with a penetrating gaze of sadness and threw himself. The dogs yelled out, "Hey, Mr. Caesar! Hey, Mr. Caesar!"

When the dogs came back, they found the Chief Pigs still assembled. Saddened by the news of Mr. Caesar's death, they pledged to fulfill his last wishes. They gave the Chief Dogs orders to start Operation Fire-Knackers, a secret project, "the *final* solution" to the penguin problem as they saw it. Since their rise to power, the Chief Pigs had been preparing three big barns as mass slaughterhouses for penguins and other opponents.

"There is still one week before the surrender deadline; that is plenty of time," said the Chief Dogs.

Every day of that tragic week, four magnificent white birds flew passionately in the skies of Penfield and Eurainia. Sometimes, one appeared in the sky of one ranch, and the others in another. Other times, they appeared in couples. They flew over the barns where the penguin slaughter was taking place. They formed a united unit, flying relentlessly. It was as if they were trying to direct the animals' attention. The trail of black, white, red, and green tearful feathers they left was endless. No animal could figure out who they were and why they were in the skies. Everybody's urgent question did not concern the reason behind their appearance and the immense shrieks that had become a continuous deep sobbing but the reason for their having so many feathers!

While the penguin massacre continued for six unhindered days, the Partners freed ranches that Penfield once controlled, one after the other. Redfarm's dogs reached the three barns where penguins were being held. Pigeons flying high above Vladimir's detection reported to those dogs seeing hundreds of penguins waddling in three lines towards three vast barns. They said they saw penguins going into the barns but never saw them go out. They could only see the smoke of an ongoing fire from the barns' upper end. The Redfarm rescue dogs were too late. They saw only remnants of the penguin massacre. Mr. Caesar's dogs, at the sight of Redfarm's dogs, surrendered before having the chance to hide the traces of the last massacre they were executing.

A few surviving penguins described what had happened.

"Mr. Caesar's army made us stand in line to go inside the three barns, promising a reward of a feed ration for our work. Hundreds of us waddled in those lines. Once we entered the barns, ferocious dogs attacked us from the back and crushed the necks of penguins with their cruel jaws. We were lucky since we slipped inside an unnoticed ditch in one barn."

The surviving penguin shed bitter tears. "After killing the penguins, the pigs burned them there."

He pointed to an enormous pile of burning wood under a metal base."They killed my family and friends. I almost died, but you saved us!"

One after the other, Penfield's Chief Pigs tried to escape. But the Partner dogs ambushed them. The dogs killed a few while capturing others. The Chief Pigs confessed their crimes and explained how they had remixed corn with the feed of many animals of Eurainian ranches and caused the Induced Drought. Chief Bulls put them on trial and executed them. So were many of the Leaders and Chief Dogs judged and executed for their hideous crimes.

The Partners freed the ranches that Mr. Caesar conquered and returned them to their rightful owners. Newfarm's reapplied its innovative remedy against extended droughts, using a mild dose of wild-gold honey to cause moderate rain to fall. Soon enough, green shrubs, flowers, and trees were seen everywhere. A few months later, the climate and weather cycle returned to normal. Animals licked their wounds and carried on with the rebuilding of their barns, fields, and lives.

PART TWO

Midlands Sea
Cedarland
Applefield
Terrains
Mountain
River
Waterfront
Terrains
Terrains
Terrains
Pasture
Mountain River
Philadelphia
N
W
E
S
Terrains
Dryland
Terrains
Egofield
Olivea

Olivia is a ranch in the Midlands divided into three distinct smaller rectangular fields of almost equal size: the Mountain, the Pasture, and the Dryland. Smaller plots of land called Terrains divide each of them. One or more animals own each Terrain.

On the western side, the Midlands Sea coast, called the Waterfront, extends east encompassing approximately one-third of the ranch, reshaping the western boundary to a semi-circular shape. It is the most fertile land of the whole ranch.

The Mountain is fertile because it has the only river on the ranch, called the Mountain River. The Mountain is suitable for planting apple trees and raising beehives. Both a cause for celebration in Olivia.

The Dryland is an arid field where most of its animals, the *Seminoles*, prefer not to live. There is neither enough grazing fields nor enough water to drink.

The Pasture is a semi-arid field difficult for agriculture. The Seminoles love it for two reasons. First, because Olivia's leaders have turned it into a free-grazing land year long. Thousands of animals flock to it after the rainy season. It turns green with shrubs and flowers for a few weeks. Second, its center has the *Meadow of the Olive Tree*, which gives the ranch its name, Olivia.

CHAPTER FIVE

THE MEADOW OF THE OLIVE TREE

The two severe droughts that hit Eurainia had repercussions on Olivia in the Midlands. During both global droughts and WARs, its animals, known as the Seminoles, saw strange things that even the older generation of Seminole animals had never seen. They saw the sudden disappearance of one or more of the four White Mystical Birds, perched on the Tree in the center of what they called the Meadow of the Olive Tree.

Generations of Seminole animals narrated that they always nested on the Tree. They never aged, nor changed their magnificent physical features, nor colors. One or more flew away for a while but always returned. They were a mystery, and countless accounts had tried to contemplate their very existence and meaning over thousands of years. To Seminoles, there was something about them so captivating to the imagination. Their bright shining bodies carried away an inquisitive animal. Realms of creativity deepened with every contemplative effort. Still, nobody could comprehend their existence, and their very nature remained mystical to animals.

The White Birds did not resemble any bird that lived on the Animal Globe. They had long necks, vast wings, thin legs, and soft, rosy beaks. While the underside of their wings was bright white, each had a different over-wing color. They were always shining and radiating with incredible charm. Because of their distinct color and mystical nature, the Seminoles named the Birds Black Majesty, Red Majesty, Green Majesty, and

White Majesty. They nested in four specific points on the Tree, creating a rectangle between them.

A fifth bird, black, too, nested on top of the Tree. The black bird settled in the center of the circle formed by the round-shaped tree surface and the center of the rectangle created by the four mystic birds. He, too, was of magnificent elegance. He was slightly larger than the White Majesties, and his black color was as dark as night. The symmetry of his body was perfect. He had three long, blue, red, and white feathers on top of his head; they were his crown. His beak was rosy, like the four white birds, but his eyes were piercing. To figure their color out was difficult because they looked blue while at other times, they were green. The black bird's most outstanding feature was his long tail of surpassing beauty in the colors of the rainbow. The Seminoles named him Black Rainbow. They referred to the five birds perched on the Tree as the Five Majesties.

The Meadow of the Olive Tree gave Olivia its name. It stood in the center of the Pasture. It was a circular flower meadow, at the center of which stood the Olive Tree. The Tree was one of a kind on the ranch. Had it not been for older generations who passed the name on, the Seminoles would not have known how to call it. The Seminoles believed that an underground spring provided the Olive Tree's roots with an endless supply of living water to sustain it. Likewise, they believed that this water and its bond with the Tree's deep roots had a mystic presence in animals' lives on the Globe. The Tree's enormous trunk and silvery bark had three great branches that had sprouted smaller branches, replete with evergreen olive leaves growing upwards and outwards. They sprouted in such a way that they created a gigantic circular perfect mushroom-looking Tree. The Seminoles designated one of the Tree's great branches and one-third of the flower meadow beneath it as the property of one of the three main animal species living in Olivia: the sheep, the goats, and the penguins.

The Meadow was home to the most exquisite natural flowers that changed appearance and color throughout the seasons. In early spring, the Tower of Bells' purple hues rose high over the grassy knolls, pink cyclamen with their downcast heads and tiny yellow primrose, a sanctuary for butterflies. During summer, white lilies and red roses filled the air with a sweet fragrance that reached far and beyond... In autumn, layers of colored grass prepared the Meadow for the winter spurges that painted on it a yellow-green carpet, decorated with pink roses and Globe-thistle. Despite their species' multiplicity, at sunset on spring afternoons, the Meadow of the Olive Tree, with its vibrant visiting butterflies and surrounding colorful flowers, swayed within the soft breeze and provided the Seminoles with surreal serenity.

The first time the Majestic Birds disappeared was on a cloudless summer day. The Seminoles gathered around the Meadow of the Olive Tree, watching their little ones play. Older Seminoles always delighted to see the little animals playing together by the Meadow. A kid goat laid flat on the ground. The others, kids, penguin chicks, and lambs, pushed him around like a barrel long enough to make him dizzy. When he stood up, he lurched before falling again and trying another time. They took turns. The playmates giggled again and again. The older animals watching them laughed with them. Because they were fatter and easier to roll, they giggled more when they rolled a lamb or a penguin.

Suddenly, a loud noise stopped the giggling and laughter. Everybody looked around, trying to find its source. As it intensified, one penguin pointed to the Olive Tree and said, "Look, the Tree is shaking. I think the noise is coming from the top of the Tree!"

The animals turned their attention to it. The young ones, frightened, ran to their parents. In a couple of minutes, the whole ranch could hear the noise. It became more agonized shrieks.

"What is that? This is awful!" said a sheep.

"Look," said a bull, "look, I can see one of the White Majesties moving her wings."

The animals ran to the top of the hill that was near the Meadow. They saw Red Majesty crying and shrieking as if she was being tortured.

"What can we do? What is happening?"

Soon enough, Black Majesty started doing the same. Then it was Black Rainbow. He started flying upwards and downwards. He spread out his rainbow tail. A halo of rainbow colors covered the sky above the Tree. Black Majesty and Red Majesty spread their long, colored wings. They flew away on the horizon toward the Midlands Sea, leaving a wet trail of black and red feathers.

"Did you see that? Oh no! They are gone!" said one animal to the others.

When the shrieks calmed with the Birds disappearing on the horizon, Black Rainbow returned to his place. Everybody could see tears in his eyes.

The incident remained a mystery to the Seminoles. It raised more questions about the mystic nature of the Five Majesties. None of them could explain what happened.

Then a horse said, "If there is someone who could explain what just happened, it is the Elderly Penguin at the Waterfront."

"That penguin is crazy; he lives in a fantasy world!" said a goat.

"Well, if anybody has another idea, let us hear it!" replied the horse.

When nobody answered, they sent a delegation of sheep, goats, horses, and penguins to the Waterfront.

The Elderly Penguin was expecting them. He came out of the sea with a fish in his mouth. Dropping it on the shore, he said, "You must be here to ask me about the Five Majesties. Aren't you?"

"Yes," said a horse.

"What irony! That we the Elderly become relevant when

you find things you cannot explain or understand! Foolish animals! To understand, you must walk away from the obvious; you must open your eyes to the rest of the Globe! What is it you seek? Answers? I have no answers."

Sad and dismayed, they turned their backs and walked away.

As the Elderly Penguin looked again at the fish, he said, "What I can say is that over the thousands of years, the Meadow of the Olive Tree had always been there. Generation after another, the main animal species, penguins, sheep, and goats, passed on their veneration of the Meadow with its Five Majesties. They told how one or more of the Majesties had flown away but had always returned to her place. So, you should not worry. They will come back."

"What about Black Rainbow? Why is he crying?" asked a goat.

"Black Rainbow never leaves the Tree. He is the central figure of the five. He is the guardian that holds the Tree and the Majestic Birds together. Tell me, how would you feel if you lost your companions that you have known for centuries? He will continue to suffer and agonize even to the point of death! He can only recover again when he reunites with them."

The Elderly penguin was about to pick up his fish when he said, "Remember this, foolish animals; it is not the Tree. It is what lies over and beyond the Tree. As long as the Five Majesties are nesting in the Tree, the Animal Globe is secure."

Then he picked his fish and disappeared into the sea. The delegation returned to the Pasture and told the animals what they had discovered.

None of them could figure out what he meant when he said, "What lies over and beyond the tree!"

A few days later, the two Majesties returned. The Seminoles rejoiced to see the Five Majesties reunited again. Months later, they disappeared again. Then they came back another time. Their appearance and disappearance continued repeatedly.

Animals pondered on these events in their hearts, always trying to understand.

In the meantime, the drought continued in Eurainia. It affected Olivia and the Midlands, but its effects were mild compared to Eurainia. Seminole life continued, as usual, planting, harvesting, and caring for beehives. They shipped more and more honey to Eurainia.

Every morning, the different species of Seminoles arriving from the Waterfront, the Dryland, and the Mountain joined in a united singing procession of walking and waddling around the Meadow. After the march, they gazed at it for minutes, trying to take in its beauty. It never failed to dazzle and inspire them. They always hoped that someday, they would grasp its secrets. Over years of living together, they worked out that one of the dominant species, goats, sheep, or penguins, would water the whole Meadow after that marching ritual. One day, a penguin watered it, the next day, a sheep, and the next a goat. They took turns. Upon watering them, the flowers' fragrance carried them away with richness and fullness of the scent. Time stopped during this ritual, and nobody present wanted it to end. While the Meadow was being watered, the Five Majesties perched on the Tree, utter sounds of contentment, "purrs" as the Seminoles referred to them. The Meadow of the Olive Tree was the veneration, the pride of Seminoles and Olivia.

The little animals continued their games. When they felt bored with a game, they played another one of their creation. Their game options were endless. Those small animals' laughter filled the ranch with joy. Despite general living hardships faced in the Pasture and on the ranch, they provided enough stamina for the adult generation.

CHAPTER SIX

The Seminoles: Rising Awareness

A few months after the end of the first drought and Global WAR I, Mr. Otto, the Chief Bull owner of Olivia and many surrounding ranches, got seriously sick. He was ill for many years, but the Global WAR destroyed his health. Mr. Otto was not the actual owner but the ranch's tenant. Since he descended from the lineage of past owners, he thought of himself as the legitimate owner. Mr. Otto used his might and force, threats, and deception to declare his ownership as the predecessors did. Most of the ranches he owned had plenty of beehives and honey. Many ranches, especially in Eurainia, desired that honey since it formed an integral part of their feed. They attempted many times to get it using all sorts of good and evil ways. And, with every attempt, Mr. Otto's illness deteriorated.

The animals he ruled were used to having different owners for as long as they remembered. They accepted Mr. Otto because they believed he was one of them. They reduced any effort aimed at challenging any ruler's authority to the minimum. Mr. Otto died without leaving a worthy successor. Lord Marshal, the mighty Chief of Chiefs of Greenfield of Eurainia, appointed himself as landlord over Olivia, Philadelphia, and Egofield without consulting the animals living on them. He did that to ensure an unlimited supply of honey and because he was one of the wealthiest ranch owners in Eurainia. Mr. Pixner, the owner of Rhonefield, who was coordinating with Lord Marshal, did the same, appointing himself as landlord over Cedarland and Applefield.

They took those ranches with little resistance. Seminoles and the animals on the surrounding ranches led a simple life. Besides being accustomed to the change of owners, they did not want to endanger their animals by taking risks with those mighty ranches. After all, their disciplined dogs saved the Globe from the first Global WAR.

Lord Marshal, hoping to preserve peace, continued Mr. Otto's policy of managing the ranch. So, he had to accept the Seminole choice of leadership. A red bull named Mr. Springs led them. Of the bulls in Olivia, he was the only one the Seminoles elected. The owner appointed the rest of the leader-bulls. Because Olivia was never independent as Eurainian ranches were, owners and animals alike did not call Mr. Springs Chief of Chiefs, but only Chief.

He had great esteem and influence over the Seminoles. To them, he was their legitimate leader! Mr. Springs was unwilling to give owners their full share of feed, apples, or honey. And like most of the Midlands leader-bulls, he was corrupt. The leader-bulls used and benefited from animals and their labor. Over the years, they grew to own vast storehouses, where they gathered large quantities of feed, honey, and apples. Sometimes, they offered a small part of their fortune to animals on their ranches, in order to keep a generosity show going on. Mr. Springs did that. Though Seminoles knew that bulls, leaders, and Chiefs were corrupt, they were used to it. They even considered that insignificant since Seminoles were used to frugal living and always welcomed the extra food rations. Besides, they trusted the leaders' willingness to represent and defend Olivia from abhorrent and deceitful owners. Bulls enjoyed a lot of privileges with their cows and calves; of course, these were not as extravagant as those of Eurainian bulls.

As for Lord Marshal, he preferred not to intervene as long as bulls and Chiefs kept Olivia in check and gave him his expected share of the harvests.

In his opening speech as the landlord, he said, "I know you are not accustomed to having Eurainian landlords. And you still think that Mr. Otto is the legitimate owner. You must look at history to understand that even if he looks the same as you and eats the same feed you eat, he differs from me. This drought has led us in Eurainia to think creatively. Mr. Otto belongs to the time of the bygones. And I say to you, "Let bygones be bygones."

He paused, and with a deeper enthusiastic tone, he resumed saying, "As a leader of the Animal Globe, I am going to help you develop your primitive ways."

He paused again and chewed the cud.

"I will help you create a living standard worthy of the times we live in. If I do not protect Olivia, another drought, should it happen—and I hope it never will—might destroy you!"

In a private meeting with the Seminoles, Chief Mr. Springs commented on these words and said, "What he meant was, 'I do not care about you, Seminoles! All I care about is my safety from another drought, so give me my share of your food and honey.'

"Seminoles, even though Lord Marshal does not speak our language, he has done nothing so far out of the ordinary, nothing that is threatening to us. We have paid Mr. Otto a share of our food; we can do the same with him!"

The Seminoles, assured that Mr. Springs was safeguarding their interests, continued planting and tilling the land and gathering the harvest in their leaders' storehouses. Mr. Springs provided Lord Marshal with the share he thought convenient. Things were generally going smoothly.

Lord Marshal used a fraudulent policy to keep firm control over the Seminoles. He sometimes caused a rumor on the ranch that enraged and engaged sheep towards goats or penguins towards sheep. He let the quarrel escalate until he, the *benevolent* leader, intervened to resolve the dispute. This show of authority was his way of proving that his presence was indispensable.

In early November, many Seminoles worked in the Mountain, picking apples from the trees. The rest of them worked at the Waterfront harvesting barley and wheat. Horses, goats and sheep, ducks, hens, and others worked together to collect the harvest. Seminole horses had a muscular build and heavy bodies. They were polite, compassionate, tenacious, and persevering. Unlike bulls who preferred to watch rather than work, horses put their physical characteristics in the ranch's service. They took part in the ranch work. They pushed and pulled the entire day.

The two most hardworking and respected horses were Elijah and Castle. These two galloped every morning for two hours before work began. They gained a mass of muscle that was the admiration of the animals, a muscle mass that the animals counted on in times of danger. Sheep and goats stood on their hind trotters, their front trotters leaning on the trunk of trees. With their jaws opened, they pulled apples from the trees and released them on the ground.

Sheep were the dominant species of animals living in Olivia and the Midlands. They were white and had big, elongated heads. Older sheep had horns that twisted and turned to the front of their heads. They were not of first-grade intelligence and depended on other intelligent animals, horses, and bulls to explain things. They were emotional and were aroused quickly. But their zeal did not last long, only for a day or two when they adjusted to newer realities and moved on with their lives as usual.

The goats were a minor but still an essential constituent of Olivia's animals. For every ten sheep, there was one goat. Though the majority worked with sheep in the fields, a few preferred other responsibilities, like caring for and educating lambs and kids, teaching them to read and write. The goats' intellectual hard work made Olivia's Seminoles win the yearly reading competition with the neighboring ranches. Goats talked little, but when they did, many animals listened.

Ducks collected the apples while hens kept pushing them to the carts; their beaks were ideal for the job. Sampson, the donkey who always looked up to the horses and admired their strength, mustered his small muscles to help them pull carts to the storehouses of the bulls. Penguins supervised the storehouses and kept a record of what arrived there. More sheep and goats mixed the wheat and barley and then divided the rations among the animals. The rest they kept, of course, aside for the bulls. They distributed the rations to the animals at the end of every Thursday; they hoped they sufficed and nourished until the next weekly ration.

One day at noon, while the animals were taking their break, a pigeon passed a discrete message from Mr. Springs to the horses. While Lord Marshal's dogs were taking a nap later in the afternoon, the three horses present, pretending to flex their muscles, passed among the animals. They announced a secret meeting hosted by Mr. Springs in the big old barn that midnight. Each animal was to give that message to his leader on the ranch.

At midnight, the Seminole leaders made their way to the old barn. They had to pass by the Meadow of the Olive Tree. With no prior arrangement, they found themselves walking around it. Its beauty carried away penguins, goats, sheep, hens, and horses. Elijah looked at the penguins and then at the sheep and goats; they had the same gaze of admiration. It was as if they were paying tribute with their silence to its magnificence. A moaning voice from the top of the Olive Tree broke the silence. They took some steps back and looked up at the treetop. The moaning sounds turned into cries of agony.

"What is it? What is happening?" asked a penguin.

"Oh no, one of the Majestic Birds!" answered Elijah.

As their eyes turned towards her, she spread out her gorgeous wings and flew away, disappearing into the night.

"Oh no, not again!" said a sheep, "We did not even celebrate their return, and now, one of them is leaving again."

"Which one is it?" asked a goat.

"It is Green Majesty," answered Elijah. "You know what this means now! The Elderly Penguin told us that when one of them flies away, the Globe is not secure!"

"Oh no, what are we going to do? What will happen?" asked a sheep.

"Let us go to the meeting," answered Castle. "Be silent, do not make any noise!" As the Seminole leaders went past the Meadow, one of Lord Marshal's dogs woke up, he said, "It is one of those birds again, it flew away! Get back to sleep." The rest of the dogs were glad to hear that order. They returned to sleep.

Seminoles hurried to the barn in complete silence. Above the podium, three flags hung. There were black with a white silhouette of a Seminole sheep. Lord Marshal's dogs woke up, looked around, and returned to sleep.

The Seminole Flag

While animals settled, there was a heated discussion among the Bulls. A few sheep stayed at the barn's entrance to look out for Lord Marshal's dogs. The animals settled. Mr. Springs turned to them, cleared his throat, and said,

"Dear animals of Olivia,

Like you, I have just noticed the sad departure of Green Majesty. It is a tragedy to lose that exquisite Bird again. This is what we were just discussing to find out: whether her departure has to do with what I am about to share!

"I have called this urgent meeting to deliberate on our position about a letter I am holding. As you are aware, we have a new landlord. That is what Lord Marshal thinks! But he is no landlord of Olivia; I assure you he is only a temporary tenant! Our former owner Mr. Otto was sick for many years. Because of the drought, after a long, painful death, predator landlords were after his vast ranches. They divided them without even thinking of the animals living on them. We, Seminoles, fell into the realm of one of the most brutal landlords, Lord Marshal of Greenfield. He rules over many ranches on the Animal Globe.

"Lord Marshal, dear animals, is a stranger. He does not speak our language and does not share the rich heritage of our forefathers. Mr. Otto, with his vices, was still one of us. He never chewed the cud in public. We know bulls do not do that. It is not acceptable! But Lord Marshal does it deliberately all the time! Do you remember his first speech as the tenant? How disrespectful he was to us? How he chewed the cud in front of us?

The animals looked at each other, nodding their heads in consent.

"It is a fact, dear animals, that Mr. Otto was cruel and corrupt, but his skin and flesh were like ours. And despite the setbacks, our relationship with him was a positive one. We, dear friends, this little Olivia of ours is but one small ranch added to the vast ranches controlled by Lord Marshal. Earlier this year, he promised to protect Olivia with its fields and animals. We warned you he was mendacious and that he was only gluttonous for our food resources. And yet, we have done nothing to resist him or his policies. We were accommodating and silent, but there is a limit to everything. We cannot allow him to take our ranch away from us. Obviously, he has made promises to other animals, foreign penguins that call themselves Penguinists. These, until recently, lived in Eurainia. He promised them a home in our Olivia!" He said all this while lifting his hooves and panting.

The animals present, alarmed at this announcement, started murmuring, causing a distorted chorus of brays, quacks, bleating, clucking, and neighs. The noise was so loud that Mr. Springs could not hear his own voice. He stopped talking and looked at the other bulls in dismay.

Then, Shepherd, one sheep who excelled in creating slogans, started shouting,

"Away with Lord Marshal."

Castel and Elijah, known for their hot temper in such matters, sprung up with anger and yelled, "Away with Lord Marshal, away with Lord Marshal."

The sheep and goats bleated the phrase a few times when bulls walked forward and lifted their hooves for silence.

When the uproar settled, Mr. Springs said,

"You know these Penguinists; you know them very well. Over the last few years, they started migrating to Olivia from Eurainia. Before the drought, the number of migrating penguins was small. They lived like Seminole penguins in the Terrains of the Waterfront and the Mountain. We welcomed them, allowed them to stay, and even taught them how to work the land. That is what we do best; our ancestors taught us to be warm and welcoming. And we cannot but help another animal trying to a escape from slavery, torture, and murder. But ever since the first drought ended and Lord Marshal took over our ranch, their migration has become a dangerous habit instead of a getaway.

I do not want to disrespect our fellow penguins here, whom we consider family and faithful Seminoles. Still, I believe these Penguinists are not penguins. They look like penguins, but they do not act like them! Our penguins are not like them!"

Mr. Springs raised the tone of his voice, "They are not like them! These Penguinists are covetous and have set their eyes on Olivia. Lord Marshal is their accomplice."

"Away with Lord Marshal," shouted Shepherd again.

"Away with Lord Marshal," repeated the animals present.

Mr. Springs raised his hoof for silence.

"We have seen over the last few years our Terrains sold to these Penguinists. I stress the fact that they have come from Eurainia. Since their numbers started increasing, they have refused to live by our habits. They live estranged from the rest of the ranch animals. They have even encircled their fields with wooden fences.

"We paid little attention to them until today, but I believe we must open our eyes and work hard to stop them from stealing our ranch after this letter. If their migration continues at this pace, we will lose our majority in Olivia. A few years ago, to every twenty Seminoles, there was a penguin; a Seminole penguin! With this recent wave, the number has dropped. Now there are only four Seminoles to one penguin, a Eurainian Penguinist."

As he said these words, he took a broad look as his tone changed.

"Lord Marshal, our treacherous tenant, is giving goodwill gestures to Penguinists; he intends to create a home for them in Olivia."

Shepherd yelled again, "Away with Lord Marshal."

The animals yelled it even louder. When there was silence again, Mr. Springs resumed, reducing his tone and looking to the ground.

"Earlier, a few bulls indeed endorsed Lord Marshal's commitment. Yes, I admit; we are not without failing ourselves. Some bulls are greedy. But do not forget what we wanted was to do what was right. We thought we were! We supported Mr. Otto. After him, we backed Lord Marshal against those in Eurainia who caused the drought and still oppressed other animals. But now that we know the truth, we cannot support him anymore.

If penguins want a home, a ranch of their own, they should have it somewhere in Eurainia where they live now, and the climate best suits their skin. We have no objection to that. But we will never accept giving up our Olivia, despite Lord Marshal's commitment to Penguinists, to become a Penguin home. Olivia is our home!

"The time has come, and it is now, to take our destiny in our hands."

His deep tone changed into a passionate cry. He looked up straight into the animals' eyes and raised his right hoof.

"Rebellion! Dear animals, Rebellion! We must rebel; we must protect our home. We must revolt and force Lord Marshal to stop Penguinists from migrating to our ranch. We must stop the transfer of our Terrains and fields to them. We must force him to grant us our independence, as he promised and fulfilled with many other ranches around us!

"As a warning to him, we will start by disregarding our agreements with him. We will stop giving him any of our feed, apples, or honey. If that does not work, we will find perhaps more forceful means to achieve our goals."

As soon as Mr. Springs said that, the animals present, filled with zeal, shouted cries of support and made promises to protect the ranch at all costs.

Shepherd developed a new slogan:

"Long live Mr. Springs, away with Lord Marshal."

The sheep, goats, and penguins repeated it a few times.

Castle and Elijah then divided the Seminoles into smaller groups and organized their actions for the future. They returned to their stalls and cubicles at the end of the meeting before Lord Marshal's dogs noticed it.

CHAPTER SEVEN

INSURRECTION

The following day, as agreed, the animals did not show up in the fields. Lord Marshal's dogs, who were keeping watch, reported it to Lord Marshal, who in turn summoned Mr. Springs to his barn.

Mr. Springs and Lord Marshal were both descendants of a rich line of bulls. Nevertheless, they hated each other. When their eyes met, each one turned away. After a minute, Mr. Springs said, "You and I understand each other. And if it were up to me, I would not even be here, but I am here for the Seminoles' sake. We want you to stop Penguinists from migrating to our ranch and to stop the transfer of our fields to them."

Lord Marshal replied sarcastically, "I believe the next thing you want to ask me is to give you your independence!"

"You promised us independence, Lord Marshal."

"You are right; I am Lord Marshal. You do not expect me to listen to this nonsense. Now go back to the fields and have the animals work, or else!"

Lord Marshal's dogs growled.

Mr. Springs looked at the dogs. "Your dogs do not frighten us. This is our ranch, Seminoles, and you are allowing the Penguinists of Eurainia to create their home here! Olivia is not yours to give; it is ours!"

"We will see about that; now get out of my barn," said Lord Marshal with a hostile voice.

For the next few months, the Seminoles continued their disobedience to Lord Marshal's orders. They refused to give him any food rations.

Then, one day, while standing on a high hill, Castle noticed a sheep listening in from behind a hedge to instructions Elijah was giving to other sheep. The sheep ran away. Before Castle could get to him, he had informed Lord Marshal about Elijah. Castle did not expect such a quick response from Lord Marshal. The latter sent his dogs after Elijah and the sheep. A pack of twelve menacing dogs arrived at the scene, looking for them.

They ordered them to surrender, but Elijah, being a hot-tempered horse, refused and asked the sheep to get behind him. He neighed and snorted at the dogs. The dogs formed a battle formation surrounding them from all sides. They barked and growled, and then they attacked. At that moment, both White and Black Majesty left their nests. They flew towards the battle zone. After a chaotic flight pattern and shrieks of agony, they returned to their nests. The sheep were killed. Angry, Elijah raised his front legs high up and smacked the dogs with his hooves. He killed two of them with one blow. Then he kicked with his hind legs and killed three more. The other dogs jumped on him, biting his body. Bruised and injured, he shook them off, jumped over a high fence, and escaped. A goat informed Castle of what had happened. Castle was furious. He tracked the spy sheep and knocked him dead with one blow. Lord Marshal, enraged, sent two more packs of his dogs after Elijah and Castle but could not find them.

As time passed, it became clear to the Seminoles that their non-violent rebellion was not achieving much. Lord Marshal was not intimidated since he managed to get his feed and honey from the neighboring ranches. He and his Chief Bulls continued to sell Seminole lands to Penguinists, whose migration from Eurainia continued with no hindrance.

Elijah's wounds healed after a few days. Mr. Springs instructed him and Castle to organize the animals for an offensive on Lord Marshal's storehouses at night. Elijah led Seminole horses and a few sheep with Sampson the donkey, pulling a cart. The Seminoles sneaked under the hedge and came to the path leading to the storehouse. Elijah jumped over the fence and ran towards the dog sleeping at the door, and with a sharp kick, he dropped him dead. The Seminoles ran into the storehouse and attacked three of Lord Marshal's watchdogs. They killed two of them, but the third ran away. They loaded the feed they found onto the cart, and Sampson pulled it to another Seminole barn.

When Lord Marshal heard about the break-in, he could not stand it anymore. He needed to get rid of Elijah permanently. He had not only brought reinforcement dogs from Greenfield, but he also had allied with Penguinists to punish the Seminoles.

Six months later, the skirmishes between Lord Marshal's dogs and Seminole sheep continued sporadically. Then Elijah and others ambushed a group of Lord Marshal's dogs, killed them, and fled to the Mountain. A spy sheep reported Elijah's whereabouts to Lord Marshal.

"Get me that troublemaker of Olivia at once," ordered Lord Marshal.

Two dozen dogs surrounded the cave behind the fence where Elijah and two Seminoles were hiding. They called him to come out. Elijah refused to surrender. He told his fellow dogs, "If we surrender now, we might live a few days more. They will take us to Lord Marshal, who will execute us anyway. So I say to you, if we must die, let us die honorably as fighters for the liberation of our ranch!"

He charged out of the hole, neighing and kicking. Enemy dogs were falling one after the other. He then threw his heavy body, crushing their leader. He yelled, "Olivia, I give you my life."

The two Seminoles attacked, as well. After a brief battle, they were both killed. Then, Lord Marshal's remaining dogs jumped at Elijah. They bruised him, but he kept fighting, killing ten of them until he had no more power to resist. Two of the dogs aimed for his neck and snapped it brutally.

Three sheep from a nearby land heard the vicious fighting. They hurried and saw what was happening. One of them ran to get help. The other two, petrified, kept a distance. They waited until Lord Marshal's dogs left the scene. Then, they approached and found the two dead Seminoles and Elijah. They could not help but cry when they saw the vicious wounds on Elijah's body.

One of them said, "He does not deserve this; all he tried to do was to defend Olivia from Lord Marshal's gluttony. We lost an outstanding leader."

A few more sheep, two goats, and two horses arrived. There was nothing they could do but show respect and sorrow. The animals pulled the bodies to the cave where they were hiding earlier and buried them there. They sealed its entrance, planting a tombstone. Mr. Springs wrote on it, "Elijah, a great hero, honorably killed here, together with two other Seminoles, in the battle for the freedom of Olivia."

They ran to the main barn and reported to the other Seminoles what had happened. Elijah's brave death provided resilience and a heroic example to the Seminoles. They continued their struggle, which turned violent trying to protect their ranch, but their horns and hooves were no match for the powerful jaws of Lord Marshal's army of dogs.

One day, Lord Marshal's dogs spotted Mr. Springs, who went into hiding after hearing about Elijah's death. They chased him until he crossed the border to the ranch of Egofield. From there, he escaped to Penfield, the safest place, away from Lord Marshal and his dogs. Caesar welcomed him as an ally since both hated Lord Marshal and saw in him a common enemy. The Seminole rebellion continued for a few more months, but without leadership and organization, it led to nowhere.

The end of the Seminole rebellion coincided with the beginning of the second Global WAR, initiated clandestinely by Mr. Caesar and Eurainian penguins' maltreatment. The number of penguins escaping from death to Olivia increased, contrary to what the Seminoles demanded. So, Seminole sheep and dogs increased their sporadic battles with Lord Marshal's dogs. Lord Marshal had to handle simultaneously the Seminole rebellion and the more significant threat of Mr. Caesar that resulted in grave anguish to the penguins of Eurainia. For the Seminoles, Lord Marshal was the villainous tenant of Olivia. For Eurainian animals, he was the ostentatious protector of Eurainia and of the penguins. With the Partners, his rigorous effort reversed the effects of the drought and the WAR and put a decisive end to Mr. Caesar and his Chief Pigs.

Lord Marshal's brutal dogs calmed things in Olivia and restored order at the hefty price of many dead Seminoles. Mr. Springs remained in exile serving Mr. Caesar. The few remaining bulls were too young to face Lord Marshal. The fighting killed most combatant male horses and rams and left the ranch with only the females and the little animals. Only Castle remained from the fighting horses. Lord Marshal's dogs searched diligently for him. He went into hiding in the Mountain. Aware that alone he could not do much, he waited until an opportune time. The sheep and goats, having nobody to lead them, had their enthusiasm expire.

Upon arrival to Olivia, migrating penguins had only one choice: to join the Penguinists. Ben, the Penguinist leader, welcomed them as brothers and sisters, for he needed their help and support.

He said, "First, you must cleanse your body and increase your skin's resilience to the rays of the sun. Then, you must undergo Penguinist education and self-protection training."

Upon their arrival, he had them immerse in a unique solution prepared by Penguinists, known as the Penguinist Bath, for twenty minutes.

During the immersion, Ben said to them, "Now, you must do this once every year. This solution will offer your skin protection from the rays of the sun for one entire year."

Ben hid from them that he added a secret medicine to the same solution that worked on their brain cells to make them more receptive to Chief Penguinist orders. He knew too well that even though penguins lived in groups, each penguin was very independent. Both males and females preferred to make independent decisions and do what they thought fitting! Yet Ben knew better. He wanted them to do what he thought was right for the Penguin Ranch! The secret medication was ninety-five percent successful in countering any independent-decision perspective. These penguins, now Penguinists, became part of the foundational force to realize the dream of a Penguin Ranch.

Ben made sure to pass this secret on to the succeeding Penguinist leadership.

CHAPTER EIGHT

REDEMPTION, STIMULATION PRE-ESTABLISHMENT

Young Ben, a Humboldt penguin, migrated to Olivia with his parents from Streamforest while Mr. Otto was still ruling it. He built his way up the Penguinist leadership. Short, with an extra round belly, Ben had very thick eyebrows. He was very intelligent and a had a commanding character. When he wanted to make a point, he had a way of scratching his belly with his wings and moving his thick eyebrows to energize and command every animal to action. He was a master architect, a decision-maker, and an eloquent speaker. His presence swayed Penguinists, and they found it hard to ignore any of his orders, for they knew of his sincere love for penguins.

Herman indeed died without realizing his safe-haven ranch for penguins. Still, his dream of establishing it never subsided among his followers. Penguinist generations continued developing his thoughts into action plans. They never forgot the Penguinist flag and the three key words he taught them: Redemption, Establishment, and Stimulation. Penguinist leaders divided their effort into different but very synchronized groups. A waddle traveled around Eurainia to stimulate penguin support to create the "Penguin Ranch." After Mr. Caesar's assumption to power, it found many listeners, and Eurainia became an unattractive place for penguins. Many penguins migrated to Olivia because of their work. Another huddle specialized in seeking resources for the redemption and building the Penguin Ranch, purchasing Terrains, constructing cubicles and fences, and preparing squids and krill ponds in Olivia. The idea of creating a Penguin ranch swayed a rich Emperor penguin called Richmond. He stepped in and provided the means. The Penguinists appointed him as the benefactor of Penguinists.

A third waddle led by a King Penguinist called Ghandi rallied support for the Penguin Ranch among Eurainian Ranch leaders and Chiefs. He succeeded with a Wild Goat named Lloyd, who was a powerful assistant to Lord Marshal and influential to Olivia's ruling policies. Unlike other goats, Wild Goats of Eurainia were lazy goats who did not want to work for their daily feed rations. They suffered from nearsightedness and could not see much beyond their noses. These characteristics led them to deviate from a set of beliefs conveyed by generations of goats on the Animal Globe about the Master-Fish. Goat species believed in a Master-Fish who waddled on the Animal Globe thousands of years ago. Goats maintained that the Master-Fish could waddle because he was a metamorphosis of a penguin. Long ago, he had hatched from a Chinstrap penguin mother living in Olivia.

The Master-Fish, therefore, had only features of fish but, in fact, was a penguin. He lived in Olivia, serving its animals. He did amazing things. One day, he went on a journey. Still, earlier, he had promised his followers that he would return to the shorelines of Olivia. To their dismay, he kept the date of his return vague. Upon his reappearance, goats believed that a green grazing Pasture would cover the Animal Globe, and animals would not have to work ever again for their food. That idea of no work swayed the lazy Wild Goats. Because they were nearsighted, every time they looked at the black penguin silhouette of the Penguinist flag, Wild Goats imagined the figure of the Master-Fish. To them, that flag was an unmistakable sign of the nearness of the Master's return.

Goats, specifically the Elderly Goats, believed that the Master-Fish concealed his return date for a reason. Every follower of the Master-Fish should emulate his service for the common benefit of animals. According to his teachings, "What you receive for free, give for free." For Wild Goats, given the Animal Globe system of life, nothing was for free. Animals had to work to receive. They could not reconcile themselves with the work concept. So, Wild Goats like Lloyd believed they could advance the hour for the Master-Fish's return to free themselves from work. In their belief, they needed to create the right circumstances for such a return.

Also, in their opinion, since their Master looked like a fish, fish-eaters had to settle in Olivia. His chances were better if more fish-eating penguins settled there. Such an exceptional theoretical interpretation obsessed their thoughts; it compelled other goats to call them Wild Goats. Blinded by such beliefs, Lloyd used his authority to hasten penguin migration to Olivia and help them buy Terrains. Ben welcomed Lloyd's passionate support. For him, Lloyd was a splendid portrait of the three words Penguinists worked for: Redemption, Establishment, and Stimulation.

Ben focused his attention on implementing Herman's motto, Establishment. He picked a waddle of devoted intelligent Penguinists to help him. Ben called them Chief Penguinists. He synchronized his work with Ghandi, who focused on the other two words, Redemption and Stimulation. Both Penguinist leaders believed that to establish the Penguinist ranch, they needed to synchronize their Eurainian and Olivian efforts. Ghandi traveled, swimming in the Midlands Sea between Eurainia and Olivia to do his important work. Ben, while in public, stopped referring to Olivia as Olivia but changed its name to the Penguin Ranch. He changed the names of Penguinists to echo a more germane connection to the Penguin Ranch rather than Olivia.

"This will have a dual effect," he told his Chiefs. "Penguinists will be more attached to the land where our ancestors waddled. And the eyes of goats, geese, and ducks, but notably those of Wild-Goats will become even more blurry and confused. They will support us even more."

The changes he introduced were a success. They continued to draw the support of different animal species, goats and Wild-Goats, who believed that their Master-Fish was a penguin.

Ben chose Moses, whose former name was Hawser, a migrant from Streamforest, as one of the Chief Penguins. Moses's job was to promote full domestic penguin-Penguinist cooperation. His primary focus was to convince the Chinstrap Seminole penguins to join the Penguinists. He met with their leader Abraham, but to no avail.

Abraham rebuked him critically. He said, "You, Ben, and Penguinists only look like penguins but do not act like us! You symbolize deformed and earthly penguins since you do not follow the Principles of Penguism, particularly the one that instructs penguins to eat only fish. Shame on you, how dare you? Eaters of krill and squids, how dare you to deviate from Penguism? Shame on you! Why are you even here? You will fail; how dare you even talk to me?"

Moses ran out in dismay and tried to focus on his other duties. He was in charge of Terrain acquisition. While doing his job, he proved to be highly ingenious in designing slogans for any purpose. His first slogan was, "In the Penguin Ranch, penguins have new hope."

Ben picked Joshua, whose former name was Jorgen, a migrant from Penfield, as a Chief Penguinist. Joshua was to head the Information; he had to know as much as possible about the Seminoles. Ben needed to verify their numbers, find their chiefs, figure out their strengths and weaknesses. He wanted to learn their feeding habits, the number of their barns, their useful agricultural terrains' locations, and the horses' and rams' fighting capabilities. It took Joshua years of dedicated work to gather all that information.

Joshua used to waddle in the fields and barns of Seminoles, pretending to have a friendly conversation with them. He asked them about their little ones, their education, and what they did in their leisure time. Sometimes, in his discussions, he spread a rumor that sheep were fighting with each other or with goats in a particular area. The hidden purpose was to find out who of their leaders was prone to intervene.

Joshua provoked sheep to talk about Lord Marshal:

"Certainly nobody, no Seminole can stand up to him; he is mighty and powerful!"

A sheep answered, "Elijah and Castle will defeat him; his time will come!"

He then used the given information for further provocation and investigation. He shared this information with other Penguinists under his command. They, too, found effective ways to observe and to get the Seminoles to talk. They kept and thoroughly documented the information.

After a year of information-gathering, Joshua tackled a significant obstacle. The Seminoles suspected the inquisitive questions of Penguinists and stopped welcoming them altogether. Information-gathering became more urgent, especially after the Seminole rebellion began against Lord Marshal, sparked by penguin migration. To overcome this obstacle, Ben and Joshua found an ingenious way. The first drought and the Seminole rebellion had caused the death of many sheep. After three months of their burial, the facial skull skin remained intact. Under the cover of darkness, Joshua and twelve King Penguinists waddled to their burial places. They dug out the tombs and took the skulls of recently dead sheep. They also took the skin coats of the sheep. With seawater treatment over five days, the skin coats and the skull heads looked alive.

In the meantime, Joshua chose a group of healthy Emperor penguins to train to walk on their fours, just like sheep. They had to use their wings as hooves. At first, it was tough, and they bruised their wingtips. But with ongoing trials, the wings became like rocks. When they had mastered the walk, they slipped the sheep skulls over their heads and the skin coats over their bodies. This way, there were twelve pretend "penguin-sheep." Joshua gave them the name "Seminole-Penguinists." They became an integral part of the Penguinist Information Strategy. Two of them, Barak and Deborah, excelled in their roles and gathered valuable knowledge about the Seminoles. Joshua made them his closest assistants. Both recruited Seminole sheep and goat collaborators skillfully, who traded information for only an extra ration of feed. The Penguinist Chiefs had to coerce other Seminoles for cooperation.

Over these years of migration and preparation for redemption and establishment, life for Penguinists in Olivia flourished, while that of penguins of Eurainia faced per-secution, even extinction. With the help of Richmond and Lloyd, Moses purchased more Terrains for Penguinists in Olivia. They used them to plant wheat and barley and to keep beehives to produce honey. In the early days of Penguinist migration to Olivia, Penguinists employed Seminoles to till and plant the fields. Once the Penguinist learned the proper ways of tilling and planting from Seminoles, they developed their methods and created newer, better, and improved ones. In no time, they stopped employing Seminoles and only used Penguinist labor. They sold the harvest they produced to Seminoles, to Lord Marshal, or loaded it onto boats and shipped it to other ranches in Eurainia. They did the same with the honey.

In exchange for this food, Eurainian animals taught Penguinists the latest progressive Eurainian ways of information gathering, and provided them with tools and techniques for digging squids and krill ponds. They taught them to build fences and tall towers. Eurainians called their newest technology "mud-bricks." In these, leftover hay, composed of the chaff of wheat, was mixed with wet soil. They then placed the mixture in wooden squares of equal size and left them to dry in the sun. A few days later, they removed the wooden squares and collected the square bricks. With this innovative method, Penguinists built more Euraianian-like cubicles in the Waterfront and the Mountain of Olivia.

The Penguinists developed a life based on a communal sharing of food and work called the *Collective.* In it, Penguinists invested their creativity in planting and harvesting. There was no Penguinist more valuable than another. They were equal in sharing the workload. To keep the Collective well under his control and well indoctrinated in Penguinistism, Ben ordered every Collective to have a private Penguinist Bath. Penguinists continued to immerse in it once a year for twenty minutes. Eurainia marveled at the Collective since penguins had never worked in the field. Yet, they were excelling at it and were even teaching the Globe innovative techniques. Animals from Eurainia flocked to Olivia to see the Penguinist achievements and learn from them. Olivia became a more convenient place to live.

Penguinist achievements, as good as they were, never could quiet Ben's worries about penguins. During the second drought and Global WAR II, pigeons brought daily news of more penguins suffering in Eurainia. His heart ached with every loss of a penguin's life. The increasing number of Seminole sporadic attacks on Penguinists in Olivia only boosted that feeling. As he aged, he developed an even more excessive paternal relationship with them. He was always distressed and carried the weight of penguin safety upon himself.

After days of deep thought, he called Joshua and his two assistants, Barak and Deborah, to a secret meeting. He said to them, "First, thank you for your continued commitment to the penguin cause. Deborah and Barak, Joshua told me how creative you are in gathering information. I am honored to have you on my side. From now on, you three, together with Ghandi and Moses, are my inner circle of decision-makers; you are Chief Penguinists."

The three of them congratulated each other with nods and step dancing.

"Second, we must realize this ranch at all costs. It will be a haven for penguins! We must prepare assault plans for the eventual redemption of Olivia from the Seminoles and Lord Marshal. We have to train every Penguinist for battle! This will be the fight of our lives; we need to master the art of attack!"

Barak asked, "Why should we learn to attack? We need to learn to defend and not attack."

Ben answered, "Attack is the best defense."

Barak then asked, "But we are penguins. We do not have the jaws of dogs, the horns of bulls, or the hooves of horses. How can we attack?"

"I have enlisted the services of a smart fighting dog of Lord Marshal's army. His name is Windsor. He loves us and hates Seminoles. He will train us to attack and defend."

As the meeting ended, Barak, skeptical of the plausibility of penguins becoming killers, thought to himself, "Ben must be out of his mind; penguin fighters! Impossible!"

Moses developed a new slogan: "Defend or be killed." He had it written everywhere in penguin-Penguinist Terrains in Olivia.

Windsor wasted no time. He started training Penguinists to become killer machines. He taught them at Lord Marshal's dog training facilities scattered throughout Olivia. In the beginning, he kept the matter of his penguins' training a secret from Lord Marshal. After months of training, Penguinists showed outstanding results, and Windsor told Lord Marshal. He persuaded him that these Penguinists would help him in his efforts to defeat Mr. Caesar should he come to Olivia.

Windsor taught the King and Emperor Penguinists how to turn their beaks into weapons to kill. First, he found particular cleavages in rocks that fit Penguinist beaks. These holes were coarse enough to act like sandpaper. Each Penguinist, male and female, kept moving their beak left and right, back and forth in the hole until it was knife sharp. Then Windsor taught Penguinists how to combine their dashing sea-to-land thrust into an assault method. His intention was to use their newly formed sharpened beaks as attack knives to pierce other animals' bodies.

"The sharpened knife-beaks," he said, "will either kill at once the assaulted animal or cause a deep wound that would still be fatal."

Years of training passed, and the Penguinists became a powerful and disciplined army. When Ben saw them parade, he was filled with pride and satisfaction to see their heads high up and sharpened beaks ready. Skeptical Barak was no longer doubtful. As one of those trained himself, his body was full of energy and combat confidence vying to come out. Ben saw his potential and made him Chief of the fighting Penguinists. Lord Marshal was so impressed with their capabilities that he made them a special unit of his army. Ben called the group of his fighting Penguinists Huddles, since he could not have an army.

He confided to Barak, "What we need now is the right moment!"

One afternoon, a few pigeons arrived from Eurainia. They announced to Seminoles and Penguinists alike that the Eurainian drought and its associated WAR had ended with the surrender of Penfield and the death of Mr. Caesar. They told of Mr. Caesar's fire-knackers, where thousands of innocent penguins waddled to their brutal end. The entire Globe was rejoicing at Mr. Caesar's defeat. They expressed how richer ranches transported feed to the poorer ones and how a fresh wave of hope promised a better future for the Globe's animals. As the pigeons told these things, the Majestic Four Birds returned to the Meadow of the Olive Tree. Black Rainbow rejoiced at their return, flying up and down while spreading his rainbow tail.

Penguinists and penguins in Olivia rejoiced in the defeat of Mr. Caesar. But they grieved the tragic loss of thousands of their species. This convinced them, especially Ben, that creating the Penguin Ranch in Olivia would definitely resolve penguin persecution in Eurainia.

CHAPTER NINE

THE BATTLE FOR OLIVIA

Individual Seminoles, frustrated and angry with the continuous, unrestricted influx of Penguinists from Eurainia, began a novel approach. They started sporadic harassments and attacks directed at Lord Marshal, but mostly towards Penguinist Terrains and Collectives.

Following such conditions and to merge their decision power, Penguinists elected Ben as their exclusive leader in Olivia a few months later. They held a ceremony and gave him a new name as a sign of respect and gratitude for his continued and relentless work towards establishing the penguin ranch. From that day onwards, they called him Old Humboldt.

Old Humboldt, always concerned for penguins, saw the sad news of the penguin fire-knackers in Eurainia as an excellent opportunity to advance the penguin ranch's cause in Olivia. Wanting to exert pressure on Lord Marshal to give him Olivia, he ordered Barak to target his attacks on Lord Marshal's dogs scattered in the Terrains and all over Olivia. Until that time, Penguinist attacks had more of a retaliatory nature against Seminole attacks targeting their fighting rams, bucks, and horses.

Lord Marshal did not know how to react to Penguinist attacks, knowing that he sanctioned Windsor to train them. He was very much aware of their tragedies in Eurainia. He, therefore waited and did not retaliate. Again, individual

Seminole horses and sometimes enthusiastic sheep and goats attacked his dogs. Lord Marshal's dogs arrested or killed the perpetrators. Negotiations with Seminole leader bulls calmed the hostile spirits. The situation deteriorated again. More assaults happened, and many animals from every species in Olivia were killed. To every attack started by Seminoles, there was a counter-attack from the Penguinists. Lord Marshal's dogs suffered from assaults from both sides.

After months of violence, it was impossible to tell who started what. Lord Marshal, as the tenant-landlord, could not leave his dogs under such attacks without retaliation. He had the responsibility to bring things under control and to restore order. He ordered hundreds of Seminoles' arrests, detained hundreds of Penguinists, and stopped their training in his facilities. But Old Humboldt did not back down. He had a backup plan: creating Penguinist own training facilities.

And contrary to Lord Marshal's expectations, Ben gave orders to further escalate Penguinist attacks on Lord Marshal's dogs, his storehouses, and even food carts. Penguinists continued their skirmishes with Seminole fighting rams, bucks, and horses. This held for another six months.

During that time, penguin migration from Eurainia to Olivia went on. Penguins had to go through the Penguinist Bath immersion and training. They then joined Barak's waddles.

In summer, a group of Penguinists led by a slim young King Penguinist called Marvin broke away from the ranks of Old Humboldt's waddle.

"Old Humboldt's strategies are too slow and too tolerant of Lord Marshal," Marvin told his followers. "Lord Marshal is bruised! We need to strike him where it hurts most. Then, and only then, will he give us Olivia!"

He planned to attack Lord Marshal's main barn in the Pasture, near the Meadow of the Olive Tree in the center of Olivia. Many of Lord Marshal's Chief Bulls lived there.

Marvin convinced his followers, saying, "If we get rid of

Lord Marshal's Chief Bulls and senior dogs in the middle of his home, I am sure he will change his mind!"

In the early morning, Marvin attacked. Dozens of Penguinists, in organized groups, dashed at everyone present in the barn. They invested no effort or interest to find their victims. The killing was sporadic. They injured and killed Lord Marshal's Chief Bulls, Leaders, and dogs, as well as more innocent Seminoles. Even though Old Humboldt condemned the attack, he continued his pressure strategies on Lord Marshal.

The Seminoles continued their random attacks on Lord Marshal's dogs and Penguinists. They learned from the experience of neighboring Philadelphia and Desertfield. Both of these ranches got their independence from Lord Marshal a few years earlier. Seminoles thought that persistence and even forceful demand would grant them their independent ranch from Lord Marshal. They continued demanding the fulfillment of his promise, to give them their independent ranch of Olivia. After Marvin's savage attack and the Seminoles' constant pressure, Lord Marshal knew he had lost control of the ranch. He decided it was time to give up Olivia and return to Greenfield.

While Lord Marshal planned how best to carry out his decision, most animals around the Globe were putting tremendous effort into understanding how and why the drought and the two WARs happened. There were many sad and embarrassing feelings of guilt in relation to the thousands of penguins' tragic end in Mr. Caesar's fire-knackers. What could animals have done early on to stop the drought from happening and to stop Mr. Caesar? Was the Eurainian punishment to the animals in Penfield for causing the first drought so severe that its animals chose Mr. Caesar? Why did Mr. Caesar slaughter those innocent penguins? Could it have been stopped? The ranches' animals were adamant that such greed and hate that Mr. Caesar showed should never occur again.

As a result, the Chief Bulls of the emerging winners in the

WAR, Newfarm, and Eurainia, agreed to elect a special council. They called it the United Ranch Council, or the URC. The URC was to promote peace and security among the ranches on the Animal Globe. It included most of the Globe's ranches. It had a special division, called the Assembly, comprised of the five leading victorious ranches, known as the Partners in the WAR. The Partners, Newfarm, Rhonefield, Greenfield, Redfield, and Eastland were the ranches that subdued Penfield and ended the drought. These five had the executive power of the URC. They had to coordinate and cooperate unanimously on everything since each one of them had rejection power.

Soon after the penguin tragedy, Chief Bulls and Elderly Goats on the ranches of Eurainia introduced a continuous process of teaching the love of penguins to animals to give justice to penguins. But they knew it would be many years before penguins felt that love. Eurainian animals' feelings of guilt were so overwhelming that they felt the need to do more. There was also pressure from rich Penguinists and Wild Goats. The URC's golden opportunity to compensate the penguins and redeem Eurainia from its guilt had come with Lord Marshal's decision to leave Olivia. They thought they should partition Olivia into two ranches, a ranch for the Penguinists and a ranch for the Seminoles. Upon hearing the word partition, the Seminoles boycotted the negotiations, objecting to the principle.

They maintained, "Olivia is our home. It has been our home for thousands of years, and we are the majority. Even after the huge Penguinist migration, the ratio of Seminoles to Penguinists is still three to one."

Old Humboldt welcomed the partition plan since he and the Penguinists owned only scattered Terrains in Olivia, amounting to a total of one-fourth of the Waterfront size. It took the URC nine months of discussions. At the end of Autumn, The Council voted to divide Olivia into two ranches almost equal in size. The Waterfront and the Mountain were to become the Penguin ranch, and the Pasture and Dryland the

Seminole ranch. The URC planned to declare the Meadow of the Olive Tree, the ranch's symbol, to be under the URC's direct supervision.

Early next winter, Old Humboldt assembled the Chief Penguinists in his Red Barn on the Waterfront. He told them, "I am satisfied with the land partition, but I am not that happy with the land allotment. I want the Dryland to be part of the Penguin Ranch."

Deborah and Barak presented their systematic plans for the eventual takeover of Olivia.

"Given the information we have from Joshua, each Seminole Terrain has from one to five fighting horses. A few sheep and goats have been training and are capable of resisting and even killing Penguinists."

Barak said, "But if we kill those fighting horses and sheep, the other animals will be vulnerable. With enough threats from our side, they will leave for safety elsewhere."

Deborah resumed her talk. "And, there is of course Castle, the horse who has gone into hiding. We know he is planning something."

Old Humboldt answered them, "We will deal with Castle when he turns up. As for your plans, keep working on them. For now, instruct your fighting waddles to adopt an 'Aggressive Defense' strategy. Concentrate on the fields that the United Ranch Council gave us!"

Moses went around the Penguinist Terrains shouting, "Aggressive Defense." Penguinists understood what the order meant. It meant that they were to retaliate with a decisive blow to every Seminole attack by destroying the place and expelling its Seminoles. Fierce fights with Seminoles increased. But neither sheep horns nor horse blows matched the organized knife-beaks and the special training of Penguinists. Barns and storehouses, and Terrains on both sides were burnt and destroyed. A few Penguinists but more Seminoles lost their lives. Penguinists expelled hundreds of Seminoles to neighboring ranches. Many

Seminoles fled to safety in the Pasture.

Even though Penguinists were better trained and outnumbered fighting Seminoles, Old Humboldt instructed Ghandi in Eurainia to circulate the news that Penguinists were losing to Seminoles. Ghandi and his assistants visited Eurainia and Newfarm. They inflated the report saying, "If you do nothing to help soon, penguins will walk the path to the fire-knackers again."

Many Chief Bulls and animals around the Globe sympathized with and were compassionate to the penguin cause. They trained penguins and allowed them to migrate to Olivia to join the fight.

Four bitter, tense, and violent months after the passing of the URC's partition plan, Lord Marshal declared mid-May as the date he would terminate his tenant-ownership over Olivia. He announced that his dog army and administrators would pull out when the date was due.

Old Humboldt assembled the Chief Penguinists for a secret meeting in the Red Barn. He first had a private gathering with Barak and Deborah for a few minutes. They briefed him on the last changes they had made to their plans. After approving them, the three joined the other Chiefs. Barak introduced the newest members he approved to Old Humboldt, who welcomed them to the Chief's inner circle.

When they settled, they heard a sharp noise outside that penetrated every corner of that barn. It sounded like agonizing shrieks. They ran to the windows. Unlike any bird they had ever seen before, they saw four gorgeous white birds flying in circles around their barn. Each Bird was flying in a random and opposing direction from the others; they almost collided. Penguinists looked at them with shock and bewilderment.

One bird, with her dazzling white color, changed her circular flight course. She directed her head to the higher clouds and flew upwards to a high altitude. Then, she threw herself in a free fall with no willingness to move her wings. Her body twisted over and over as she headed towards the ground. Just before hitting, she spread her wings and flew straight into the window of the Red Barn. The collision injured her head, but she resumed her flight and joined the other three birds. The Penguinists saw her sad features and her lovely eyes welling with tears. As the four birds flew away, the Penguinists saw a trail of four colors of wet feathers.

For a few minutes, they pondered who those Birds were and why they were in agony. Terrified and amazed, they looked at each other, asking questions. Both Old Humboldt and Joshua knew the answer but did not move.

Joshua said, "These are the four Majestic Birds perched on the Olive Tree in the center of Olivia. The Seminoles said they do that sometimes, but that is not our concern! Let us get on with our meeting."

Old Humboldt focused on his speech. He scratched his belly, raised his thick eyebrows, took a sweeping look at the attendants, and said,

"Fellow Penguinists,

Lord Marshal is leaving Olivia in two months. This is our best opportunity to realize our dream ranch. Our forefather Herman envisioned it, and now it is up to us to make it a reality. However, unlike Herman, who believed that we could buy our ranch over the years, it is clear now that his way will be a laborious process. And perhaps we will not achieve our goal because, after dozens of years, we have only purchased scattered Terrains.

"Penguins have been suffering for ages. We have family and friends Mr. Caesar slaughtered in Eurainia. How long will penguins have to walk the path to the slaughter?"

He paused, scratched his round belly again, raised his eyebrows up and down, and tapped his feet; everybody's attention was on him. The older Penguinists knew well he was going to announce something significant.

"We have an opportunity now to become free of the tyranny

of animals, and we have to seize it. Many ranches around the Globe are ready to recognize our ranch!"

He continued scratching his belly, rocking from side to side, and moving his thick eyebrows up and down.

"But there is a price we have to pay for our freedom. We must be strong beyond imagination. Yes, we, the oppressed penguins of the Globe, must give up our moral code for a short time. Penguinists must do what we never thought a penguin could do.

"We must use unpitying cruelty against the Seminoles. We have to do it, as harsh as it sounds; it is the price we have to pay if we want our ranch."

Everyone who listened to him was in awe. Silence overtook them. After the Four Majestic Birds' loud ordeal, one could hear a needle drop in that barn.

"The Seminoles have to make way for our ranch. They are three times greater in number than penguins. They will never give up their homeland for our sake. Without extreme force, they will not leave. For them, it is their Olivia. For us, it is our Penguin Ranch, and it is our right to create our ranch there. No matter how much we try to explain it to them, they will never understand penguins' suffering. They have to leave, and we have to take their place. We have no other choice! It is the right thing to do!"

"What do you mean by 'they have to leave?'" asked one of the new members, breaking the spell of silence.

"It means that we shift strategy, going from "Aggressive Defense" to an ""Aggressive Offense" strategy. We must exert enough pressure on them using all means: fear, intimidation, expulsion, and even aggression. We just want them to leave; we have to make them leave!"

Another new member asked, "Where will they go?"

Old Humboldt answered, "We will always have an open escape route for them. They can leave to Cedarland, to Applefield, or Philadelphia, or anywhere else. I am sure that the ranch owners around us will be more than welcoming to a few more of their species! They can resettle in the Pasture; many sheep live there. The few penguins who live there consider themselves Seminoles; they do not wish to be on our side. And besides, that field is only good for grazing goats and sheep! Our settling there will demand our investment of our valuable resources into creating the right environment for penguin life."

Some Penguinists welcomed his declaration with no hesitation. They looked at Old Humboldt with nods of satisfaction. But he troubled others. They could not believe that to achieve their freedom meant to act in that manner. Deep inside, though, being the executors of his orders so far and witnessing Seminoles' resistance and their attachment to their land and barns, they knew Old Humboldt was right. They had to do it! In that meeting, and despite the unsettling feelings, Penguinists decided that time to adopt a systematic offensive plan had come, the plan of an "Aggressive Offense."

Penguinist waddles, led by Moses, Joshua, and Barak, moved from Terrain to Terrain and from barn to barn, horrifying Seminole animals. They gathered the colts, bucks, and rams outside their barns. They had the "Seminole-Penguinists" and their collaborator Seminoles sort the fighting Seminoles among them. Penguinists lined them up and then slaughtered with the sharp beaks of the King Penguinists in front of the others. Any Seminole who dared to defend himself or his family shared the same fate. From that point, Penguinists adopted different approaches with the remaining Seminole animals, depending on the information Joshua had gathered earlier. Some were released when Penguinists thought their terror was enough for them to flee from their barns. If they thought the Seminoles would not run away, they expelled them. In both cases, after the Seminole exodus or expulsion, Seminole barns, Terrains, and belongings were burnt so that they could never return.

In the larger Terrains, surrounded by vast wheat and barley plots and under the solid administration of a Chief Bull, the

Penguinist plan was to burn the surrounding plots. Those Terrains' storehouses were soon running out of feed. They allowed an animal a food ration only if he left to a neighboring ranch's border. Richer Seminoles were the first to accept such a proposal since they owned other fields and barns in neighboring ranches. They took their families and friends and fled to them, with the hope, of course, to return after the conflict. This terror, expulsion, and voluntary transfer went on for days, and thousands of Seminole animals left Olivia.

Old Humboldt ordered Penguinists to further escalate their attacks on Lord Marshal's army of dogs. Simultaneously, Marvin's break-away raft conducted raids on other barns owned by Lord Marshal at the Waterfront. They freed his Penguinist friends held there and slaughtered two of Lord Marshal's Chief Dogs. They left their bodies in the center of the barn.

Days later, a pigeon reported to Castle, the Chief Horse, news of the ongoing Seminole tragedy. He was still in hiding from the wrath of Lord Marshal. Troubled, he wanted to avenge the Seminoles. He gathered fighter Seminoles, sheep, goats, hens, colts, horses, donkeys, and even pigeons for the battle. The day arrived in early spring.

Castle chose a crucial path that connected the Waterfront fields to the Pasture. Seminoles, who controlled it, depended on Sampson, the donkey, and other horses to pull the feed carts from the Waterfront to the Pasture. Since the Penguinist attacks had increased a few months earlier, the Seminole Chief Bulls had them escorted by a few fighting dogs and sheep. Two days before the chosen date for the battle that Castle was planning, a waddle of Penguinists had taken the hillside opposite to that path and expelled its Seminole animals. The Penguinists were preparing to ambush Sampson's convoy when Castle arrived at the head of his compact unit of fighting animals. Admired and respected by every Seminole for his courage and resilience, he assumed full command, realigning the fighting horses and sheep in three consecutive lines. He ordered his dear friend

Sampson to stay behind to protect the carts with two other horses.

At dawn, Castle marched in front of them and almost attacked the Penguinists on the hillside when Sampson stopped him.

"I want to charge with you. I have great hooves, and you need all the help you can get."

Aware of the seriousness of regaining complete control of that path, Castle allowed him to join the attack. They charged at the hillside with all their might. "For the liberation of Olivia!" Sampson shouted, striking left and right with his hooves. He killed a Penguinist in one blow and injured three more. The colts and sheep charged and killed a few more. With his colossal size and big muscles, Castle alone went through the ranks of the Penguinists, kicking left and right unopposed. His thick trotters killed many Penguinists.

Then the Penguinists regrouped their lines and yelled, "For the freedom of the Penguin Ranch!"

They pressed together at the edge of the hill and dashed at the Seminoles. Their combined dashing weight was enough to throw Castle, the horses, and the sheep down the hillside. Then within a flash of a second, they dashed on them again, aiming their knife-beaks straight for their throats and slew them. The pigeons flew back to the Pasture and reported the news of the battle to fellow Seminoles. Dozens of other sheep and colts ran to the hillside. The Penguinists, outnumbered, gave up the hillside and fled in the Waterfront's direction.

The Seminoles found the dead bodies of Castle, Sampson, and the others. With Castle dead, they lost the will to continue. They knew that without him, their defense was no match for the organized Penguinist offense. The next day, hundreds of Seminoles arrived at the scene. They pulled his dead body and buried him on the hillside where he died, together with Sampson and the others. They called the battle and the hillside after him: "The Battle of Castle."

Just after that, Red and White Majesty uttered a sharp agonizing cry. When there was enough attention from Seminoles and Penguinists, they flew in circles. They then turned towards Marvin and his break-away Penguinists, who were hiding and watching what was happening from a distant hill. Marvin was planning to use Castle's burial ceremony to execute an attack on a Seminole Terrain. The two Majestic Birds left a trail of white and red feathers over them. Though puzzled, Marvin was not moved. As the two Majestic disappeared on the horizon, he gave orders to attack the Terrain, butchering innocent sheep and goats. Among those slaughtered were lambs, kids, and pregnant ewes.

News of this calamity spread in Olivia by Penguinists and by Seminoles. As for Seminoles, they passed the word with panic, hoping that the neighboring ranches would come to their aid and rescue. The Penguinists' primary intention was to terrify Seminoles and cause them to flee. Marvin's raft terrorized Seminoles, yelling out, "Leave or share their fate!"

For their safety, many alarmed Seminoles fled towards the Pasture and Olivia's borders. The outcome was a continued mass exodus of Seminole animals. Old Humboldt condemned Marvin's massacre. But the Penguinist strategy of "Aggressive Offense" succeeded in forcing the Seminoles to leave.

CHAPTER TEN

ESTABLISHMENT-PENGUIN COLONY

Lord Marshal faced an impossible situation of his own creation over the years of being a landlord to Olivia. He wanted to become the Midlands ranches tenant-landlord, rich with honey that Greenfield's animals needed, thinking he was doing the right thing for his ranch.

As a result, he had to make promises and concessions, whether to Olivia or to its neighboring ranches. He promised the Seminoles an independent ranch in Olivia but did not keep his promise. Consequently, they never ceased to challenge his authority. He underestimated their determination and attachment to their land. He also had the penguins, another group of simple, long-suffering but dedicated animals. To ease their suffering, they, too, wanted a ranch of their own. He helped them migrate to Olivia, promising them the creation of their independent ranch there. The Penguinists were definitely going to make him fulfill his promises. He underestimated their attachment to their cause.

As the tenant-landlord, he had the responsibility of keeping order. With his authority challenged and attacked from both conflicting sides, he shifted sides the whole time. It depended on who was exerting more pressure on him. As time passed realized that the Seminoles, though more in number, were losing to the well prepared Penguinists. More than once, they requested his intervention on their behalf to no avail. He refused to act. Unless there was a real danger to him, he refused to react against the Penguinists the way he had responded towards the Seminoles a few years earlier when they rebelled against him. He found it inappropriate to subdue the Penguinists, specifically after what penguins went through in Eurainia. Lord Marshal watched the Penguinist offensive on the Seminoles and did nothing to stop it. He set his eyes for departure!

Because of his inaction, one-fifth of the Seminole animals were expelled or fled for safety. Half of the Seminole Terrains were burnt, and hundreds of their barns were emptied. More Penguinists continued to migrate from Eurainia. During these events in Olivia, Ghandi and his assistants continued their campaign to recognize the Penguin Ranch. They concentrated their efforts on Newfarm and Redfield. After the second drought and WAR II, the whole Animal Globe viewed both ranches as the Globe's new leaders. Old Humboldt told Ghandi, "Their recognition could inspire many other ranches to do the same."

The day for Lord Marshal's departure arrived. On the same day he lowered his banner, Old Humboldt, commanding total Penguinist control of most of the Mountain, the Waterfront, and the Dryland of Olivia, raised the Penguinist flag. It was the same flag Herman had chosen for Penguinistism years ago, white cloth with a silhouette of a black penguin in its center.

Old Humboldt had two of these flags hanging in the Red Barn center, at the Waterfront, just above the podium, as he went to deliver his speech.

In the presence of hundreds of Penguinists, he said,

"The Penguin Ranch was the birthplace of penguins. Here penguins shaped their uniqueness among all creation. Here they had their first ranch and created a way of life necessary for penguins and the Animal Globe. From here, we gave the Animal Globe decent rules for animal life.

They forced us out of our ranch for generations. But we have never lost our connection and yearning to reestablish ourselves as free animals in our ancient homeland.

In recent decades, penguins seeking a new life away from Eurainian Ranch persecutions have migrated to the Penguin Ranch. They have made it bloom again. They have revived the ancient penguin language, built and renovated Terrains and Fields, and brought progress to the animals living in it.

Our father Herman proclaimed our right for a ranch of our own; Lord Marshal recognized it with his announcement of establishing a Penguin Home. The United Ranches Council recognized the penguins' past connection with the Penguin Ranch and confirmed our right to build a Penguin Home. The United Ranches Council called for the creation of a Penguin Ranch; it required its animals to take steps to achieve that end. From here, I confirm to you that this recognition of the United Ranches Council of the right of penguins to establish their Ranch is permanent and irreversible."

He moved left to right and scratched his belly.

"The calamity that penguins faced in Eurainia is another affirmation of the urgency of creating this Ranch in the Penguin Ranch. We open its gates to penguins from all over the Globe. Here they can live in peace and freedom and without fear!

Accordingly, we representatives of the penguins in the Penguin Ranch, and Penguinists around the Globe, on this day of the termination of Lord Marshal's custody of the Penguin Ranch, by virtue of our deep connection to this ranch, ratified by the power of the United Ranch Council, declare our independent penguin ranch, called Penguin Colony."

An overwhelming step-dancing and powerful nodding overtook the attendants. The penguins cried with joy. Moses shouted, "Long live Penguin Colony."

Everybody repeated after him. They felt at last liberated

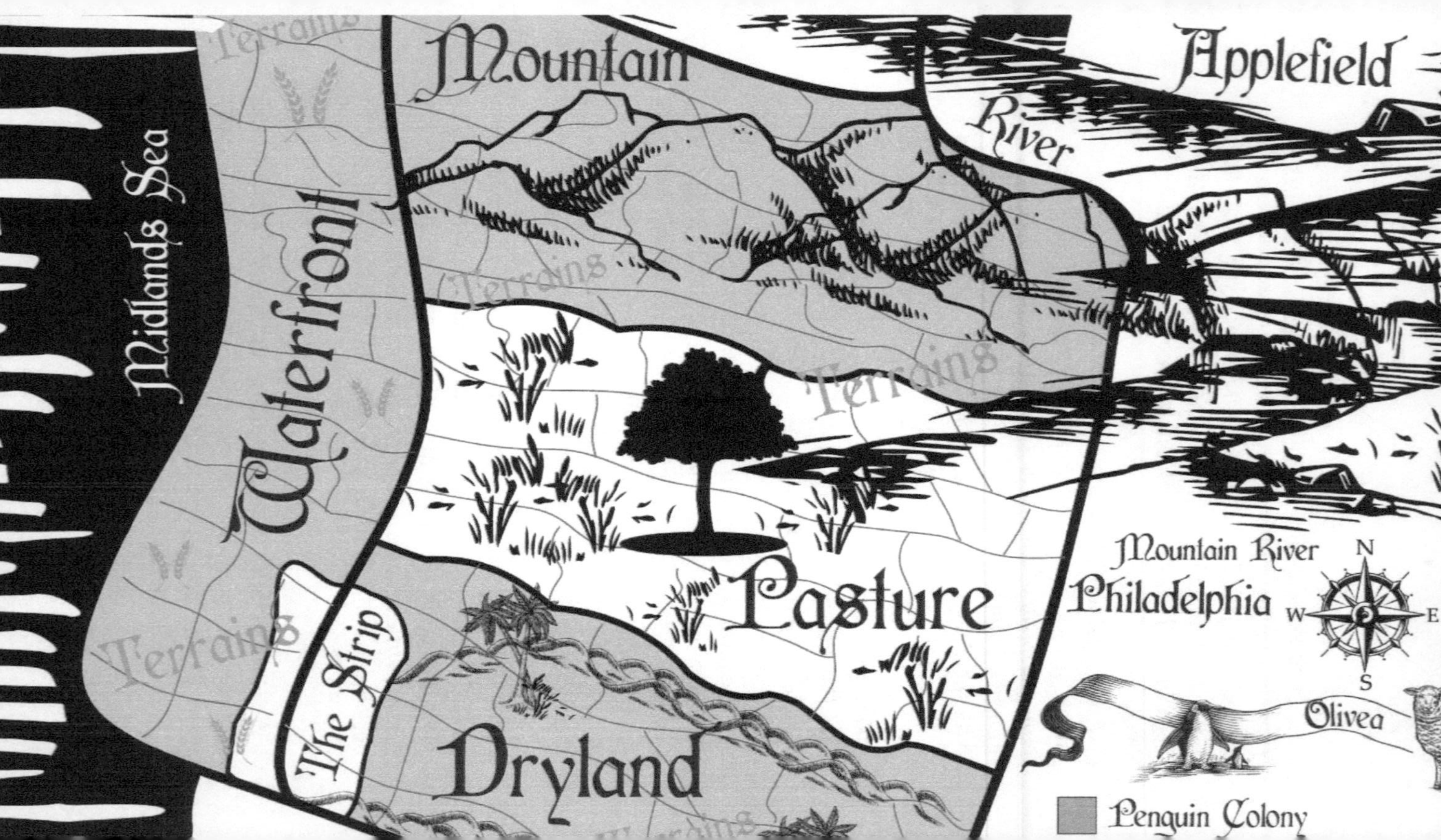

Mountain
Applefield
River
Midlands Sea
Waterfront
Terrains
Pasture
The Strip
Dryland
Mountain River
Philadelphia
N
W
E
S
Olivea
Penguin Colony

from anxieties and persecution. They were free penguins in their own ranch. News of this declaration spread immediately to areas under Penguinist control. They rejoiced with dancing and humming.

Then Old Humboldt signaled for attention. When there was silence, he said, "Our fighting waddles are to be united into one army: the army of Penguin Colony Defenders (PCD). They will be under the command of Joshua from today. Now, before we adjourn this meeting, let us sing the Penguinist hymn. A fellow Penguinist wrote it years ago. I believe it is appropriate, and we should adopt it for our cause and Penguin Colony."

As four young penguins mounted the cloth that had the words on the wall of the barn, he began singing.

"Penguins of the east, penguins of the west, penguins, penguins all over the Globe, rejoice, rejoice, rejoice.

Our hope is alive, as ever as it was; a ranch of our own, hundreds of years alive, penguins, penguins all over the Globe.

Penguins of the east, we pledge to work hard, Penguins of the west, we pledge not to give up the right, the right above every other right.

Penguins of the east, penguins of the west, we will have a life, free from any strife, in our own ranch, we will create, once in the penguin ranch.

Great shall be the world we sow, for all the animals on the Globe, they will achieve even more, for our success is the success of them all.

Penguins of the east, penguins of the west, rejoice, rejoice, rejoice."

The solemnity of the tune caused the zealous Penguinists to calm down. A few of them picked up the melody and started humming it. Others were in tears while singing it, for they felt a rejuvenated hope for a better future for penguins in Penguin Colony. They were so carried away with the hymn that they sang it over and over.

The first to recognize Penguin Colony was the ranch of Newfarm. Redfield recognized it a few days later. Old Humboldt and Ghandi continued their hard work around Eurainia and Newfarm, approaching bulls and Wild Goats to strengthen the new born Penguin Colony. They were very successful, and more ranches in Eurainia recognized it.

The neighboring ranches to Olivia, Egofield, Cedarland, Applefield, Philadelphia, and another ranch further north, Desertfield, would certainly not recognize Penguin Colony. They were furious with the declaration. They sent hundreds of dogs, sheep, and goats to rescue Olivia and the Seminoles. Egofield sent with its dogs a herd of Wild-horned Rams who hated penguins and Penguinists. The Chief Bulls released them from prison to join the fight for Olivia's liberation.

Cedarland sent dozens of fighting dogs, but their mission was to safeguard its borders with Olivia if Penguinists attacked it. In spite of that, Penguinists occupied a few Terrains in Cedarland, which they returned after the fighting was over, and an agreement was reached. Applefield and Desertfield sent more dogs than sheep but were not as disciplined as Penguinists.

The most disciplined and well-trained army of those ranches was that of Philadelphia. The other four ranches appointed Philadelphia to lead their offensive against Penguin Colony. But they did not know that Philadelphia's Chief Bull, Cain, known for his wit and foresight, had already concluded a secret agreement with Deborah, a Chief Penguinist. He had met with her twice before Old Humboldt's announcement. Of the Chief of Chiefs in neighboring ranches, Cain was smart enough to know that the Penguin Ranch was inevitable and would be created under any circumstances. So, he tried to obtain as much as was possible from the prevailing conditions. Greedy to capture the Pasture and its Meadow, Cain made a secret agreement with Deborah that the Penguinists would let him take it. In return, he promised that his participation in the assault on Penguin Colony would be minimal. In their last meeting, as he felt that Deborah was rescinding their secret agreement, he threatened her. "Don't you dare try taking the Pasture!"

He instructed Desertfield dogs to protect the northern side of the Pasture. His army covered the center and the southern sides.

As to the other two armies of Applefield and Egofield, they did their best, rushing through the border with loud cries: "Death to Penguin Colony, go back to the sea!"

Enthusiastic about joining the attack, they were confident of their victory. But the two armies underestimated the power and organization of Penguin Colony. They advanced and seized a few Penguinist Terrains and barns, only to lose them again later. Upon arriving at the Waterfront, Chief Dogs and sheep, who feared for Seminole ewes and lambs' lives, ordered them to leave their barns. It was a precautionary measure to save their lives until they forced the Penguinists back to the sea. The ewes took their lambs with hens, goats, and bucks and followed the orders. They ran away, only to find another fight and another battle. They kept running and found themselves at the borders of Olivia. It soon became clear to the Chiefs that though they were more in number than Penguinists, neither hooves, horns, nor jaws were as deadly as the disciplined Penguinists' and their sharpened beaks. They were also so disorganized, not to mention deceived, that they could not drive the Penguinists back to the sea. Soon enough, they lost the battle for Olivia.

Old Humboldt divided his PCD army into two, one that defended Penguin Colony from those armies and another that continued to force the Seminoles to flee. The recent arrival of Penguinists from Redfarm added much more power to his army. He ordered them to engage Egofield and Applefield. The others dealing with the Seminoles, Old Humboldt ordered to hasten their operations. They continued going from Terrain to Terrain, barn to barn, gathering rams and bucks, killing their leaders and expelling the rest. Their fields and barns were burnt and destroyed.

Old Humboldt did not communicate the truth to his army engaged in battle in one Terrain about other battles elsewhere. He always gave the impression that unless Penguinists fought harder, they could lose and walk the fire-knackers' path again.

Moses produced another slogan: "Kill or walk the path." It inspired every Penguinist. They attacked with courage and pointed their beaks at their enemies, even under the most stringent circumstances. Penguinists, caught in isolated barns and surrounded by dozens of enemy sheep and dogs, fought and prevailed, inspiring more fighting courage in other Penguinists. Old Humboldt made sure that such heroic news spread both on the ranch and everywhere. Ghandi played a crucial role in transmitting to the Globe's animals the penguin battle for survival. Likewise, he used the same rhetoric for the principal global Ranch Chiefs.

"We are fighting for our lives; help us, or the penguins will walk the path to the fire-knackers again."

After a few days of fighting, Old Humboldt, confident of the Penguinist capabilities on both fronts, gave orders to attack the Pasture field to capture the Meadow of the Olive Tree. The PCD waddles arrived and tried to capture it. Cain was adamant about not letting them take it. His most ferocious of dogs with jaws very wide surrounded the Meadow. A few Penguinists tried to approach but had their necks broken in seconds. So, the Penguinists pressed together in groups of dozens and charged. The bitter fight killed many on both sides. After various failed attempts, the Penguinists retreated to the Waterfront. They continued fighting and repelled the attacking armies from the three fields they took from the Seminoles, the Waterfront, the Mountain, and the Dryland. They expelled most of the Seminole animals who lived there or had them flee for safety.

Newfarm and then the Assembly of the URC intervened to stop the fighting. After various failed attempts, the Assembly nominated a goat named Bernard to mediate between the sides. They appointed him because he successfully mediated agreements between Penfield and Eurainian Ranches during the second drought. The ranches involved in battles welcomed him. Penguin Colony received him with delight because it remembered how he had saved hundreds of penguins from the fire-knackers. Bernard proposed that the URC re-partition Olivia in half. Penguin Colony was to allow the unconditional return of the Seminoles who fled because of the fighting. A Penguinist raft led by a Penguinist called Isaac slaughtered him the following day of submitting his proposal.

Bernard's successor continued the work based on the newer realities—Penguin Colony's total possession of three fields—and reached a truce a few days later. Fighting animals retreated and returned to their ranches. Half of the Seminoles lost their fields and barns to Penguin Colony, and Olivia ceased to exist. From that day on, it became known as Penguin Colony.

From the Meadow of the Olive Tree, Black Majesty gave a loud and sharp cry that every animal heard in Penguin Colony. Both Seminoles and Penguinists saw her flying over the ranch, and her agonizing voice echoed for days! Many goats in Eurainia reported seeing her a few days later flying over Eurainia, but nobody understood why! Migrants and fleeing Seminoles to Eurainia reported they had not only seen her fly over Eurainia but had heard her disturbing cries for days. When these Seminoles asked the United Ranch Council and its Assembly if they could see her and hear her voice, they said, "We have seen her but could hear nothing!"

In private talks, the URC leaders said, "This is the right thing to do!"

A few days later, Black Majesty disappeared from the skies of Eurainia.

PART THREE

CHAPTER ELEVEN

Penguin Colony-Success Story

After the Penguinist victory, Old Humboldt convened another secret meeting of his Chief Penguinists in the Red Barn. When they gathered, they sang the national hymn. Then, they started step dancing and nodding their heads joyfully, congratulating each other on a job well done.

Old Humboldt, formally recognized as the Chief of Chiefs in Penguin Colony, said, "Congratulations, Olivia is ours. Without your dedication and tremendous effort, we could not have created Penguin Colony so swiftly. Everything we have dreamed of and planned for is now a reality. You should be proud of yourselves!

"A few years ago, penguins were walking the path to the fire-knackers, helpless and stripped of everything. They had no way to defend themselves. Our fathers' tragedy has taught us that penguins should never allow another animal to lead us again to the slaughter. You, Chief Penguinists, and the Penguinist army have stood up and defended thousands of penguins from walking the path. WE HAVE DEFEATED MR. CAESAR!"

A pandemonium of blissful humming went on for a few minutes. Then Old Humboldt started scratching his belly and moving his eyebrows.

"The Animal Globe has learned a solemn lesson from the past two droughts and Global WARS. Ranch owners keep a close eye on events happening in different parts of the Globe.

They do not want another Global WAR to happen ever again. The price paid by animals was beyond imagination. I am sure that they will prevent another tragedy like the one that befell us from happening.

"So, we have to be careful and plan our future steps well if Penguin Colony is to endure. I know penguins had to pay a heavy price that will doubtless weigh on their conscience for years. Breaking the Principles of Penguism, the principles of our forefathers, and the deep heritage was necessary and inevitable; yes, it was a heavy price to pay to create our ranch. But I want you to calm your hearts and know that everything that happened to the Seminole animals is justified and had to be done. This is the price we had to pay for creating our ranch, and they, sadly, had to pay for being on our expected ranch.

"The worst is behind us now. We have to build on our achievements and the global animal scene and keep building our dream ranch: a flourishing place and a safe haven for penguins on the Animal Globe. I have put together a few guiding principles we need to follow. I have called them the Ten Commandments of Penguin Colony, the Ten Commandments of Penguinistism. Herman's teachings and dozens of years of experiences inspired them. Learn them, follow them, and teach them to your chicks. Remember, though, these commandments are ours only and should not be shared with any other animal.

1. *Denial of any connection to the Seminole tragedy.* We will deny responsibility for the tragedy that befell the Seminoles in front of the Globe. The Seminoles fled on their own, and their allies, the neighboring ranch owners, ordered them to leave!
2. *Denial of Seminole right of return.* Seminoles cannot return to their former barns or fields. We will be under pressure from the United Ranch Council to enable their return; we will declare our good intentions but will never comply.
3. *Seminoles were never here.* To make sure that they never

return, we need to wipe out, as much as possible, any memory of Seminole animals living on this ranch. We will continue to destroy their barns, burn their Terrains, and build on top new penguin barns and water ponds or plant trees. Make sure you give the new barns and their surrounding areas our ancient heritage names. Remind the whole Globe always and diligently of our justified presence in Penguin Colony.

4. *Constrain remaining Seminoles.* The Seminoles who managed to, or we allowed to, stay in our ranch, we must constrain to minor Terrains and barns. We will not allow them to move or expand beyond our geographic plans.

5. *Win the Chinstraps.* We still need to win the Chinstrap penguins to our side. Give them the fish they ask for. Learn and encourage the adoption of their feeding and breeding habits. On these issues, Penguinists can yield to penguins; after all, we are penguins, and Penguin Colony is the Penguin Ranch.

6. *Every penguin is welcome.* Any penguin who wishes to return to Penguin Colony is welcome. We will encourage penguins everywhere to migrate to the Penguin Ranch.

7. *Follow a Progressive Legal Framework.* Everything you do has to be legal and progressive. Everything we do towards building our ranch is to be done in a legalistic system. Our law will have to justify and defend our doings in front of the entire Animal Globe.

8. *No penguin is to trust other animals.* But, if other animals serve our needs, we will welcome cooperation with them.

9. *Wild Goats are our allies.* They are lazy and nearsighted; their beliefs mean nothing to us. We will welcome any cooperation with them as long as it supports our cause.

10. *Enhance Safety.* The last and most important thing is that the Penguin Ranch must always be safe. Nine commandments are one thing, and this one is another. The safety of the Penguin Colony is of the utmost importance. Every pen-

guin, male and female, must learn how to defend this ranch. Our Penguin Colony has to be the strongest.

"If Penguin Colony is to prevail in the Midlands, this is the right thing to do...."

At that moment, there was a disturbing noise heard outside. This time, Penguinists rushed out. Old Humboldt, seeing that there was no one left in the meeting, followed them. They saw Red Majesty flying in circles over their Red Barn. It looked, though, that blood drops stained her white body. As she flew over the barn, she was crying with grief and deep sorrow. One teardrop fell on Old Humboldt's head, who, for a moment, looked disturbed by the agonizing voice but pretended to be aloof. As he wiped the tear from his forehead, Red Majesty disappeared on the horizon.

He asked everybody to disregard what they had just seen and to return to the meeting. To most, it was hard to focus on what was being said. Many Penguinists kept thinking of what the apparition of Red Majesty meant. Old Humboldt paused and reconvened the forum in the morning.

The following morning, the Penguinist Chiefs reappeared at the meeting. They looked sad and deprived of sleep. Old Humboldt overheard them talking to each other.

"This cannot be happening; this is not who we are!"

Upon seeing them and hearing their impressions, Old Humboldt yelled at them, "Wake up, stop this! Do you want to walk the path again? We have work to do!"

Moses said, "No penguin should walk the path again, never again!" He repeated it three times, shouting it louder and louder. Then, they repeated the sentence after him,

"No penguin should walk the path again, never again!"

This continued for a few minutes. Then Moses started singing the Penguinist hymn. They sang it with him.

When he drew everybody's attention back to the penguin cause, Old Humboldt divided the Chief Penguinists into four groups. One group worked on abolishing physical traces of Seminole existence. It continued burning stalls and barns everywhere on the ranch. Once that happened, they built new penguin cubicles over them. Such cubicles were much needed and welcomed by recent waves of migrating penguins; many did not know what had stood there before. To them, having a cubicle of their own after a long journey of suffering and migration was more than welcome.

After burning the barns near the sea, the Penguinists dug immense pools connected to the sea by waterways they dug in the ground. They brought in seawater that had contained different penguin foods: squids, krill, and fish. Tens of Penguinists dived in and caught but did not consume the different food types and distributed them in the various pools in which they added only krill. In other pools, they dropped in krill and squids. Still, in others, they added krill and fish. In the last pools, they brought in fish only. Then, they threw in wheat and barley in the pools. Within a few months, the marine creatures reproduced, and there was food for every penguin and Penguinist. The days when penguins had to eat small rations were over. Many Penguinists tried the fish for the first time, and to their surprise, they enjoyed them. A few Penguinists added fish to their daily diet of krill. Others appreciated the fish taste so much that they stopped eating squids and krill and instead made fish their primary food. Many Chinstrap penguins, who had fled from Eurainia and migrated to the former Olivia and the present Penguin Colony, welcomed those eating fish with much affection and satisfaction.

A second group worked on the narrative related to Penguin Colony's creation. They had to continue and build upon the work by Ghandi and Old Humboldt in Eurainia. Ghandi surrounded himself with a few powerful hawks. He kept them close and well-fed with fish from fishponds. In no time, they became a fierce advocate of Penguin Colony. Now that they had created their ranch, Penguinists found it easier to concentrate on the outcome rather than the means. Ghandi distributed slogans in Eurainia and Newfarm:

"In their ranch, penguins are free from the prejudices of the Globe's animals."

"Penguins have a right to exist"

"Penguins have finally defeated Mr. Caesar."

"Penguins are heroes."

Old Humboldt, Deborah, and Barak traveled around the Globe seeking recognition of the Penguin Ranch. Chiefs received them as heroes.

"We were penguins without a ranch and created one in a ranch that had no animals," they said.

The hawks repeated these messages regularly.

Old Humboldt, in his visits to the Globe's ranches, repeated these words: "The neighboring ranches attacked our ranch because we are penguins, and they hate us! We were smaller and were outnumbered. The neighboring ranches wanted to lead us into another path towards another doom, but, with your gracious help, we have prevailed and won. Thank you for your ongoing support and assistance."

With feelings of guilt and vivid memories of penguin slaughter in Eurainia, Animal Globe was just as eager to rid its conscience of those horrific memories as the Penguinist commitment was to create the Penguin ranch. The Globe saw in Penguin Colony's creation a well-deserved act of justice. It was incapable of hearing anything but the sounds of the penguin victory.

A third group developed a scheme of rules and regulations for Penguinists to manipulate to favor Penguin Colony. The structure looked progressive and comparable to leading ranches in Eurainia but was ambiguous enough to allow flexibility for penguin control and total subjugation of Seminoles and their Terrains. Some of these rules were:

"Animals have the right to choose their Chief leaders,"

"All animals on the ranch are equal,"

"All animals on the ranch can move freely,"

"Every animal has the right to education."

Ghandi and his hawks presented these rules everywhere. The animals in Eurainian ranches hailed the penguins for their achievements.

"They are an authentic example of progressive Eurainian animal principles," said Chief Bulls.

The whole Globe was unaware that the Penguinist definition of the word 'animal' was "a penguin."

A fourth group kept itself busy with the safety of Penguin Colony. The Penguinists viewed Penguin Colony as the only progressive ranch in a region of hostile and primitive sheep-dominated ranches. They trusted no one. They understood Penguin Colony's vulnerability to reprisal attacks from neighboring animals and Seminoles who had recently lost everything they called home. Old Humboldt ordered the Penguinists to build fences between Penguinists and the remaining Seminoles on the ranch. He ordered them to dig huge and deep trenches in various border areas of the ranch with neighboring ranches, intending to repel attacks from sheep, goats, and dogs.

"In moments of real danger," he said, "we can channel seawater by opening the various dams we built for that purpose. Penguins swimming deep in the water surreptitiously can launch surprise attacks on our enemies."

The groups regularly met over many years and coordinated their work until the practice picked up its momentum; it worked in harmony and organization. Penguin Colony had become one of the most successful ranch stories on the Animal Globe. A few years after its creation, it competed with major ranches and taught them management and organization. Its army was one of the mightiest. Its capacities were superseding those of the hostile neighboring ranches together. Newfarm, Penfield, Rhonefield, and other ranches in Eurainia sustained it without conditions. Penguinists felt proud of their achievements.

Hundreds of animals on the Globe were pouring into it to see for themselves.

After a few months, Old Humboldt ordered Penguinists to plant green Eucalyptus trees, the seeds of which were brought from the Farm of Australinea. They planted them everywhere in Penguin Colony, including in the Dryland. Old Humboldt had a particular veneration for that Field with a dream of seeing it bloom. The Chief of Chiefs ordered Penguinists to dig trenches channeling water from the Mountain River, the only river on the ranch. He instructed them to bury him in the Dryland. As time passed, the entire landscape of Penguin Colony changed. There were green pastures, and Penguinist-penguin chicks played under the trees with joy and excitement.

Old Humboldt instructed Penguinists to dig deep to find any trace of penguins who lived on the ranch long ago. Soon enough, a Penguinist found a skeleton of a penguin buried in the ground. Old Humboldt called the Chief Penguinists and the flying birds and presented the discovery to them.

"This is proof to the Globe of our rightful ownership of this ranch," he said.

The Chief Penguinists were very glad for the discovery. They invited a few hawks and a few pigeons visiting Penguin Colony from other ranches to inspect it. The two pigeons inspected the skeleton.

"How can you be sure the skeleton is that of a penguin? We hardly have the spinal cord. Without the skull and feet, we cannot tell if this is a penguin or a sheep!"

The hawks, after investigating, tried to convince others it was the skeleton of a penguin. The pigeons and hawks flew and talked about the discovery they saw. The old skeleton's finding swayed many animals and started a vigorous controversy that continued to grow with every passing day. Geese from Newfarm, known for their skill in such matters, volunteered to check the skeleton. After inspection, they concluded that there was not enough to prove either of the two opinions.

The pigeons tried to tell the animals of the Globe the evidence was not conclusive. But the speed and agility of the hawks' wings that penetrated more ranches and barns suppressed their voice. Many penguins who were still skeptical of the idea of a Penguin Ranch changed their minds and started supporting Penguin Colony. They thought, "After all, there is evidence that our ancestors lived there long ago."

They visited it many time and every visit brought to its leaders' unique gifts. Finding the skeleton sated Wild Goats' appetite. Many flocked to Penguin Colony. They needed no more proof.

"The Master-Fish will appear soon, as he had appeared to this dead penguin long ago!"

As their eyes looked at the green Terrains, they saw a sign of the long-awaited times when they would not have to work ever again. They parented many orphaned Penguinist chicks in Penguin Colony and put their support and power at Old Humboldt's disposal.

Old Humboldt was satisfied with the support. But nothing pleased him more than the gift brought to him by Mr. Pixner, owner of Rhonefield: a fresh supply of wild-gold honey. Neither former Olivia nor Penguin Colony nor any of its neighbors ever had any wild-gold honey. They only had regular honey. Old Humboldt knew too well the mighty hail that could result from its proper mixing with animal feed. He remembered the time when Newfarm used it on Japaland.

"Nobody will dare attack us once they know we have this capability on our ranch," he thought. "But for the sake of the ranch's safety from the URC's inspection and heist attempts from neighboring ranches, we will keep this information ambiguous to the rest of the Globe. We will never acknowledge either having or not having it," he told the Chief Penguinists.

Years passed, and Penguin Colony functioned well. A fresh wave of migrant penguins from Eurainia brought in James, an intelligent Emperor Penguin with a visionary mind. Eurainian animal life's developments influenced his progressive character, to volunteer and to develop Penguin Colony. Old Humboldt loved his ideas and added him to the circle of Chief Penguinists. James had a new ingenious project, which Old Humboldt embraced quickly after consultation with Deborah, Barak, and Moses. The new project, called the Tower, was to carry the ranch into a new development era. He wanted to build a massive tower in the center of the Waterfront. Many Eurainian ranches and Newfarm, after the second drought and Global WAR II, had individually developed and adopted the Tower project to help each other rise from the ashes after the WAR. He explained that animals around the Globe who wished to support Penguin Colony could contribute one or more building stones for the Tower. These stones would bear the animal's name or the name of the group of animals or the ranches contributing to them. In return, the receiving ranch pledged to help and support the giver, an animal, a group of animals, or a ranch. Their pledge was to help build or rebuild a similar Tower should any of these entities fall into hardship and give them food. The presumed rule of the Tower project was to interconnect the fate of participating animals and ranches. What happens to one affects all! So, all must rally to save the one.

Even though the Tower-building itself rested on penguins, they still did not know how to design it. Old Humboldt employed expert goats from Eurainia to design it. The Tower should have window openings at various heights. An electrically operated elevator would take animals contributing a stone to these levels. The rooftop was available to nest three eagles, birds that live on a few ranches. Newfarm's Chief Bulls ordered these eagles to settle on the Tower building. Their sharp eyes and hunting skills were unmatched on the Animal Globe. They were to survey the whole ranch and its immediate surroundings.

As soon as they started the building, Penguinists realized, given their size, hauling in massive rocks was an impossible mission. James proposed to employ Seminole horses and donkeys for the job. These, at first, objected to the idea of working for penguins, but faced with the shortages of food, they accepted it. As time passed, the cooperation proved to be a success. And since Penguinists provided the Seminoles with generous amounts of feed rations, they hoped Penguinists would be more forthcoming in employing more Seminole animals everywhere. They toiled in building the massive Tower. In the summers, they worked twelve hours daily. In winters, they worked eight. Hundreds of distinct entities wishing to contribute to the Tower came and provided their shares.

The builders had brief breaks for food. Penguinists ate fish and krill brought from the pools near the Waterfront and gave Seminole horses and donkeys rations of feed. Penguinists used to dive into the water to search for their marine food at the beginning of the building project. Over time, they thought they were wasting valuable time in their search for food. That time, they believed, they needed to better invest in building the Tower and Penguin Colony.

They devised a new way of searching. A few skillful Penguinists created nets from long thin seaweed they found on the beach. After drying the weeds, they could attach them to cross stitches to make durable and wide nets using the sharpened beaks of King Penguinists. Then, the nets were let down to sink, and once they were full of marine animals, they swiftly raised them. They incorporated this system throughout the ranch. Penguinists could turn their attention to building the Tower and other needs of the developing Penguin Colony.

The Tower fascinated the entire Globe. Any mischief happening to it meant disaster; many vowed to protect it, especially those contributing a stone or more to its building. A few years later, they finished, and Penguin Colony's destiny became intertwined with that of the rest of the Globe. The ranch became one of the most robust and most developed ranches on the Animal Globe. Its development even superseded ranches in Eurainia. Ghandi and his hawks reported its achievements with unfaltering attention.

Penguin species' life was changing in Penguin Colony. From hunted to hunters. From animal seekers of help and protection to animals teaching safety, providing progressive service and development. The Tower they built brought them attention and support. Newfarm's Eagles nested on it and kept everybody in check. Penguinist agricultural production was sold everywhere. With that development, Penguinists were becoming fatter and lazier. Working the land became too difficult, too much for many. Chief Penguinists employed more Seminole animals to do the work.

Another byproduct of their achievements was that some Penguinists missed or delayed their assigned immersion in the Penguinist yearly Bath. Cracks showing in their skin and their feelings of the summer's extreme heat reminded them of the immersion's importance. And even though they were finally immersed, something strange was happening to their brains!

CHAPTER TWELVE

OLIVIA: RISING RESISTANCE, PENGUIN COLONY: SETTLEMENT

Creating Penguin Colony on Olivia led to various outcomes for the Seminole animals. It forced more than half of them to leave their barns and Terrains. Seminoles called them the Dispossessed, who ended up in four prime locations: Cedarland and the Pasture that came under Philadelphia's control. Many Dispossessed arrived at a Terrain, called the Strip, bordering the Dryland of Penguin Colony on one side and Egofield on the other. Philadelphia likewise received a large number. Penguin Colony's creation resulted in making the rest of the Seminoles Migrants and Displaced. The more privileged Seminoles, the Migrants, fled to ranches in Eurainia and Newfarm. Even though they were welcomed, they were still hoping to return to their Terrains in Olivia. They were fortunate and created a new life. The Displaced Seminoles, who stayed in Olivia, now Penguin Colony, against all odds and pressures, were subject to strict Penguinist regulations. Their food was rationed, their barns often ravaged, their education controlled, and their mobility limited to their joint Terrains.

The Dispossessed Seminole tragedy was above and beyond any Seminole's imagination. One day they had everything, and the next day they had nothing: no barns, no Terrains, no Fields, no Chiefs, not even feed for their little ones. Old Humboldt thought and hoped that neighboring ranches would be more forthcoming and accommodating towards their species, but he was wrong. In those ranches, the Chief Bulls objected to the assimilation of Seminoles in their respective ranches. They explained their point of view to Seminoles.

"As much as we desire to welcome you to our ranches, we cannot, because if we do this, it means that we are helping you give up your right to return to your original barns and Terrains. We are sure that is not what you want from us. We will keep supporting your right of return at every opportunity at the United Ranch Council and its Assembly."

The Dispossessed, from their side, insisted on their right of return to their homes. While they waited, the imposed circumstances compelled them to live an impoverished life begging for food from their host ranches and the United Ranch Council. They felt humiliated, angry, depressed, betrayed, and forgotten.

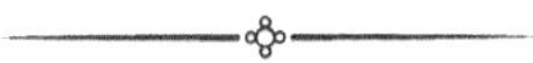

The years went by. Penguin Colony's successes overshadowed Olivia's existence in the memory of the animals on the Globe. Neither Penguin Colony, nor the Assembly or the URC, were prepared to allow the Dispossessed to return to their Terrains. And the more successful Penguin Colony was, the more resentment many Seminoles felt.

After a few years, a bull named William emerged. He was a young Seminole, slim but able and shrewd. He had a white body decorated with a strange puff of long black and white hair on his forehead, covering both his eyes. Animals always wondered how he could see in front of him. He was born in Egofield to a wealthy bull Seminole family. During the battle for Olivia, he joined the army of Egofield. He fought bravely but losing the battle always weighed on his heart. The priority of his life became giving back Olivia to the Seminoles, using the force and means he could muster.

William was popular among the Dispossessed Seminoles. Dispossessed himself, he shared with them their defiance and resentment of the Penguinist domination of Olivia. His zeal for the Seminole cause of return to their homeland forced him to go around the inhospitable neighboring ranches and encourage the Dispossessed to fight. He gave them hope that there was still a chance to win back their lost Olivia. With time, he gained many followers of dogs, sheep, and horses. He headed and launched sporadic surprise attacks from various border points on Penguin Colony, killing dozens of penguins. Though such attacks caused no real threat to its existence, they disrupted Penguinist life's normalcy and generated fear among penguins. Old Humboldt's army repelled these attacks with excessive force, killing many assailants and forcing the rest to flee. He hoped that such a lethal force would dissuade William from launching further attacks.

But this brutality did not persuade William. The opposite happened; his actions stirred many other Dispossessed to do the same. They, too, organized into small groups, launching attacks on the borders of Penguin Colony. With time, William found himself leading what Seminoles called the Resistance; it included multiple groups fighting Penguin Colony to reclaim Olivia. The slow battle with Penguin Colony persisted year after year.

After decades of service to the Penguin Ranch and years of devotional work to save penguins and build Penguin Colony, Old Humboldt died in his small cubicle in the Dryland. Just before his solemn death, he summoned Moses, instructed him on the way to use the secret substance he added to the yearly Penguin Bath, and told him, "I have dreamed of the Dryland blooming. Carry on with my dream."

To honor him, Penguinists re-energized his dream. They invested much more effort in making the Dryland bloom, planting more trees and flowers, digging water ponds, and building recreational parks for Penguinists. They buried him there, as he desired, in a unique square-shaped tomb. The Chiefs planted a flower bed over it, the seeds of which they brought from his original homeland, Streamforest. They planted a larger rectangle of green grass around it. Penguinists planted twelve tall Eucalyptus trees on every side, which provided shade for various official Penguinist ceremonies over the years. In front of the trees, they hoisted twelve masts with twelve Penguin Colony flags.

On his tombstone, the Penguinists wrote, "Here rests Ben, Old Humboldt, creator and father of Penguin Colony."

Eurainian ranch Chiefs from the Animal Globe came to pay tribute, placing flowers over his tomb.

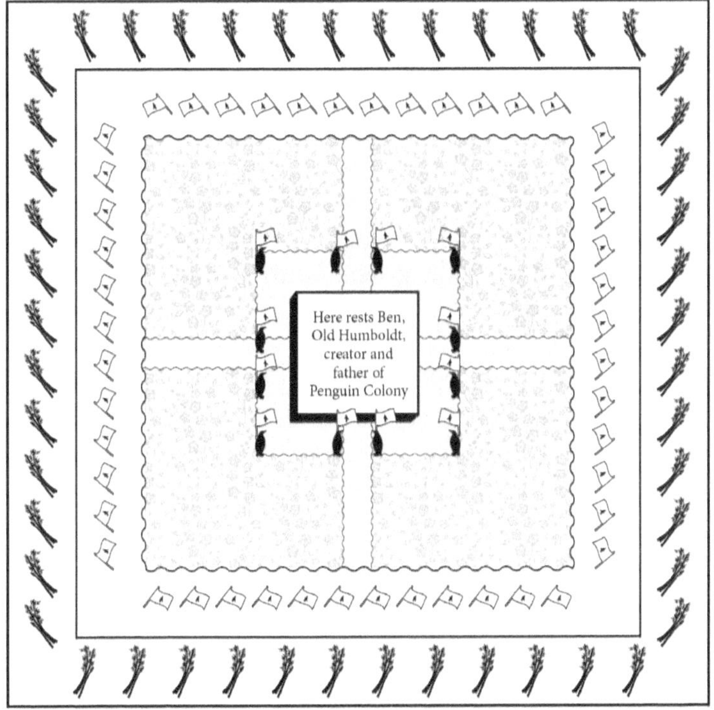

The Ceremony at Old Humboldt's Tomb Plaza

Penguinists made it a custom to visit his burial place once a year and do a commemorating ceremony. On that day, Barak ordered the flag's lowering to half-mast as Penguin Colony mourned his death. The ceremony comprised twelve young and hard-looking Penguinists standing in a straight line in front of his tomb at the edge of the flowerbed opposite the twelve trees. Each one was carrying a flag of Penguin Colony. The Chief Penguinists selected them every year from the most robust ranks of the Penguinist army. For the young Penguinists, their selection was the highest honor.

Then, the Penguinist in charge of the ceremony shouted, "Penguin Salute."

The young Penguinists waddled with the flags around the flowerbed. Then, the Penguinist in charge shouted again, "Penguin Colony Salute."

The twelve Penguinists said these words, "Penguin Colony, by the soul of our founder, Old Humboldt, we pledge to protect you. You shall never fall!"

Then, each Penguinist, in a solemn step, moved forward and placed the flag on a post set for it around the tomb. The participants then sang the Penguinist hymn, and the ceremony concluded.

Penguinists elected James to succeed Old Humboldt. After proving a deep commitment to the Penguinist cause and bringing Penguin Colony to a flourishing era, his election was obvious. And he, too, like Old Humboldt, was obsessed with the safety of Penguin Colony. He believed that the best defense was a good offense.

During one of their regular inspection flights over the neighboring ranches, the eagles living on the High Tower in the center of the Waterfront noticed an unusual massive movement of animals towards the borders of Penguin Colony from Egofield. They reported this to James, who summoned Barak and Deborah. The three, always committed to Penguin Colony's safety, did not take any chances. James gave orders to launch a surprise preventive attack on the three ranches: Egofield, Applefield, and Philadelphia. At night, thousands of penguins from the Penguinist army plunged into the Midlands Sea and the Mountain River's water. They swam until they were near their shores and riverbanks.

At the correct time, while animals were sleeping, the Penguinist army dashed out of the water and attacked their enemies. Caught by total surprise, those ranches' armies could not regroup and mount a meaningful and adequate offensive. In a matter of days, Penguin Colony not only caused a decisive defeat to its neighbors but had gained many of their Terrains and Fields. It occupied a small Field from Egofield and the Strip that Egofield occupied since the creation of Penguin Colony, where thousands of Dispossessed Seminoles lived. Penguin Colony occupied a vital mountaintop that overlooked Penguin Colony from the north side belonging to Applefield. It occupied the Pasture with its Meadow of the Olive Tree. Hundreds of Seminole animals from the Pasture fled again to safety in neighboring ranches.

The United Ranch Council's Assembly was furious with the attack and condemned it. It demanded that Penguin Colony return the Fields. Penguin Colony refused to comply, claiming that it would return them only after successful peace negotiations with its neighbors. Its defeated neighbors not only lost their Fields but also their honor. They were indeed unwilling to negotiate with their enemy until they had regained their honor.

When Wild Goats saw the Penguinist flag flying over the Pasture, it overwhelmed them with joy. To them, it was another relevant sign of the imminent re-apparition of their Master-Fish. Their blurry eyes became more dazzled every time they looked at the Penguinist flag. They promised to build more penguin cubicles, more training areas, and double the Tower's height. They had influence over Newfarm's leadership, which they used in favor of Penguin Colony. The Assembly tried to hold Penguin Colony accountable using every means possible. But Newfarm, with its economic ties and interests in Penguin

Colony, with its need for a continued supply of honey from the Midlands, and the unceasing pressure of Wild Goats in favor of Penguin Colony, used its veto power and stopped the whole accountability issue. Newfarm continued to use its rejection powers to support Penguin Colony.

James captured from Philadelphia what Old Humboldt didn't at the creation of Penguin Colony. The Penguinists rejoiced. The Seminoles wept. Not only did they have to accept Penguin Colony's rule for an undetermined period, but they had to grapple with the Penguinist claim that Olivia belonged to penguins. They thought, "Lord Marshal only wanted a share of our feed and honey. But Penguin Colony wants everything!"

A few years later, James, convinced that the Displaced Seminoles' behavior within Penguin Colony was reasonably peaceful, upgraded their status to not-quite-equal animals. That was the peak they could achieve, given that they were not penguins. Even though there were still many restrictions on their lives, they noticed an improvement in finding work opportunities and traveling to Penguin Colony's distant areas. James refused to treat Seminoles of the Pasture and Strip in the same way. He ruled them with different rules that meant to restrict and control every facet of their life.

Lord Marshal's earlier phase of oppressive rules over Seminoles inspired many regulations Penguin Colony adopted over them. They controlled education, food rations, work, Field and Terrain ownership, mobility, and barns. Penguinists dug deep water pools and trenches in many areas in the Pasture and the Strip, acting as if they owned the land and disregarding its real owners. Seminoles were not allowed to bathe in, or drink from, these pools.

Ghandi, in answering the United Ranch Council's question on the deep pools, explained, "The number of penguins migrating from Eurainian ranches is soaring. We need to build more cubicles and squid-fish farms for them. Besides, those fields are empty. Do you want more penguins to die of hunger

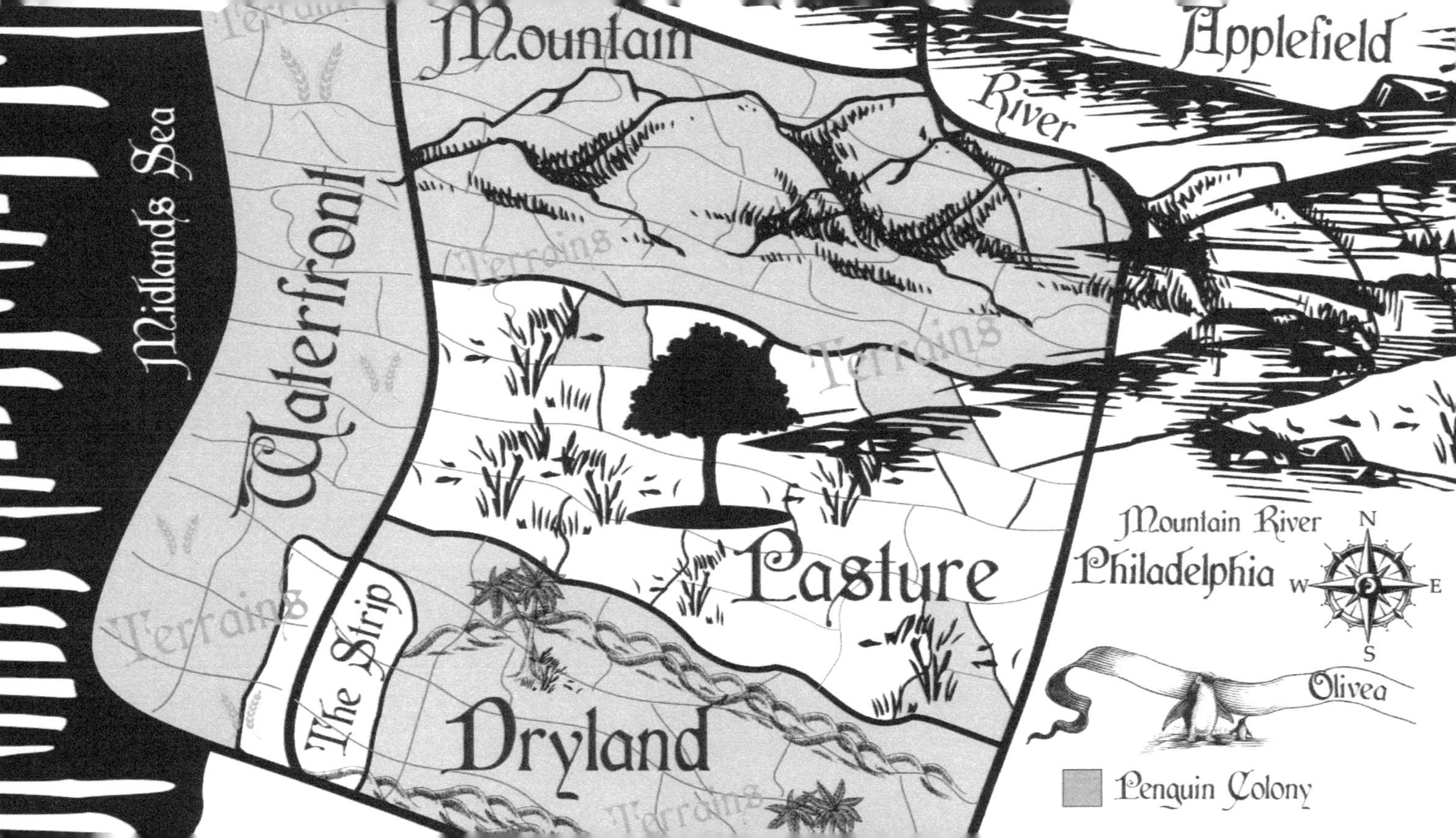

Midlands Sea
Waterfront
Mountain
Applefield
River
Terrains
The Strip
Dryland
Pasture
Mountain River
Philadelphia
Olivea
Penguin Colony
N
E
S
W

under your watch?" The Eurainian United Ranch Council Chief Bulls were fully convinced. They did not want to carry another guilt of penguins dying from hunger!

To Seminoles, these trenches were meant to isolate the Meadow of the Olive Tree from the rest of the Pasture. They tried to explain this to the URC, but to no avail. As criticism ended, the Chief Penguinists used the pools as recreation areas for penguins. More pools were spreading all over the Pasture and covered roughly one-third of them. In no time, the Penguinists surrounded these ponds with a wooden fence. It became hard for Seminole animals to move from one sector of the Pasture to another. It was even worse to reach the Strip, since most of it Penguinists surrounded with even deeper water pools, trenches, and fences. Violent skirmishes between Seminoles and Penguins were on the rise.

CHAPTER THIRTEEN

DISRUPTION:
THE MEADOW OF THE OLIVE TREE

As time went by, significant changes were happening to the penguin species within Penguin Colony. Some Chinstrap penguins who doubted the idea of a penguin ranch changed their minds upon seeing the achievements and successes of Penguin Colony. They, witnessing that a few Penguinists adopted their feeding habits, only enhanced their positive sentiments. As a result, they started rallying support for it among other Chinstraps as well.

Moses saw a golden opportunity to resume the conversation with Abraham, the Chief of the Chinstrap penguins in Penguin Colony. One evening, he knocked on his door.

To his surprise, Abraham said, "Come in. I am having a fish meal; please join me." After the meal, Abraham said, "I congratulate you for your achievements, but it seems to me that you know little about your ancestors and their principles."

Moses, still perplexed from the warm welcome, asked, "What do you mean?"

"You, Old Humboldt, James, and the rest of the Chief Penguinists, when you first came here, cited ancestral heritage in your claim to Olivia. Tell me, do you know anything about your ancestry? Do you know what it means to live a penguin life? Do you know any of the penguin principles, Penguism?"

Moses answered, "Well, I am a penguin whose ancestors

lived here in Olivia thousands of years ago. A landlord expelled them hundreds of years ago, and ever since, we have been living in Eurainia."

Abraham asked, "What about the Principles of Penguism?"

"I will learn; teach me wisdom."

Abraham reached his table and found a book. "I read many books, but if there is one book you must read, it is this one. The Principles of Penguism are in it."

He opened the book and found the text. "The teachings of Penguism are the rules concerned with penguin feeding and breeding practices and view and conduct in life.

Penguism has eight Principles:

1. One Creator created all animals.
2. All animals he created equal.
3. Penguin practices exemplify the magnificence of the Creator.
4. Penguins eat only fish.
5. Penguins do not kill other animals.
6. Penguins must promote peaceful coexistence among animals.
7. Penguins migrate for breeding.
8. Penguins' life is deeply connected to the Meadow of the Olive Tree in Olivia."

Abraham and Moses paused and looked at each other, trying to read each other's mind. Though Moses knew some commandments hearing them from Abraham had a transformative experience.

Then Abraham said, "My friend, you, Emperors, Kings, and Humboldts have disregarded many, if not all, of these rules. The only reason you are here now is that I see Penguinists changing their attitudes. I am going to give you the benefit of the doubt. I am going to assume that you did not know these principles."

Moses was about to talk when Abraham said, "Let me finish, please! I will assume that you did not know these principles and could not practice them in Eurainia. But no more. Today,

I have given them to you, and I want you to keep this book to teach Penguinists the authentic ways of penguins. Embrace the spirit of the principles and try to live by them. When I see you change, I will continue this conversation with you. Now please, leave me alone!"

Moses could not open his mouth. He was not sure how to react and did not even know whether the meeting went well! Taking the book, he left, reading and pondering for many days. Later on, Chief Penguinists shared its contents with the rest of Penguinists. Some welcomed the teachings while others did not.

Penguinists who experienced interruptions and delays in their yearly Penguinist Bath underwent sweeping side effects. Besides the skin problems, which were the more visible, a few Penguinists were becoming less receptive to Penguinistism. Chief Penguinists knew the reason, but they did not want to risk revealing their secret. They knew that the brains of such Penguinists were less affected by the secret medicine that Old Humboldt had ordered to be added to the Penguinist Bath.

The ill-affected Penguinists were experiencing various forms of mental and physical alterations. Inspecting their bodies and then the scorching sun, they remembered that their bodies looked very different in shape and size.

They asked themselves, "This sun is burning our skin. What are we doing here? This is not our normal habitat. We should not be here; this is crazy!"

Others had their brains affected. These questioned everything; they were curious about their surroundings, their neighbors, and their leadership. Some effects were so powerful that Penguinists refused to serve in the Penguinist army. A few Penguinists, now penguins, found the sea and returned to Eurainia.

Chief Penguinists, witnessing the changes, concluded that the alterations were permanent and were nothing less than the development of newer penguins species. Based on the alterations' levels, they gave the newer species names such as

Galapagos, Macaroni, and Snare penguins.

Other Penguinists, besides disrupting their Baths, had changed their diet from krill to fish-krill. These had a unique experience altogether. Over the years, they shrank in size, their body features continuously changed, and their brains underwent strange metamorphoses. Penguinistism and its Ten Commandments were not enough for them. They knew they were Penguinists and had to live by the Ten Commandments. Yet Penguinists knew similarly that they were penguins! They tried to conduct their lives by adopting both the Principles of Penguism and Penguinistism at the same time. Chief Penguinists gave this species the name Royal Penguinists. Abraham, the Chinstrap Chief, was fond of these.

Still others developed a strange connection with their forefathers. The Chief Penguinists called the new species Gentoos and Little Penguinists. They felt their forefathers' spirit, the spirit of the designers of Penguism, hovering over their hearts and minds. Many of them reported having dreams of their forefathers, pointing them to the Pasture and the Meadow of the Olive Tree. They invested time to learn the Principles of Penguism and were fond of the eighth Principle,

"Penguins have a deep connection to the Meadow of the Olive Tree."

While investigating its meaning, they discovered they were not the only Penguinists interested in it. They found out that a group of Penguinists, who arrived from Australinea, was also investigating it. The group identified itself as Rockhopper penguins who came to Penguin Colony to fulfill the sixth commandment of Penguinistism. The Chief Penguins were not aware that a different species of penguins existed in Australinea. However, being penguins, they welcomed them.

The Rockhoppers, having a common interest with the Gentoos and the Little Penguinists, spent days deliberating what that Principle meant. They knew that being Penguinists, they were to redeem the land of Olivia, this being one of the founding principles of Penguinistism. Being penguins, they needed to find out what that eighth Principle meant. They believed its meaning was that penguins had a deep physical connection to the Meadow, as their forefathers had.

They believed they needed to be physically present—resettled in the Pasture—to reveal the complete picture to them. It meant that they needed to work towards retaking possession of the Meadow of the Olive Tree. They started settling around there, although essentially no penguins lived there but a few Seminole Chinstraps. In fact, Seminole sheep and goats had lived there for centuries. The three Penguinist species moved to live in the Pasture and the Strip. Among the rest of the Penguinists, they were known as the Colonizers. A few Penguinists had sympathetic views of the Colonizers, while others loathed them. The Colonizers lived in isolation, trying to figure out ways to redeem Penguin Colony by repossession of the Meadow of the Olive Tree. They showed complete contempt for the severe objections of Seminoles living there. They challenged the authority of the Chief Penguinists as well, threatening to kill even penguins who tried to uproot them from their ancestral homeland!

Crossbreeding between different penguin species had produced newer species of penguins. Their skin was tolerating enough of the rays of the sun, showing no cracks, so that they needed no immersion in the Penguinist Bath. They stopped immersions completely. As a result, they were unresponsive to Penguinistism with its Ten Commandments or Penguism with its eight principles. Chief Penguinists called them Yellow-eyed penguins.

The habitat change from cold to hot weather affected emergent generations of Penguinists within Penguin Colony. Penguinists had different body features and different outlooks on life and approaches to living it. Their physical body changed. They gained weight, and their sizes doubled. Others had developed thicker eyebrows. Still others had their beaks swollen or shrunk, but most had a combination of changes happening to their bodies. From the original four penguin species, eleven new ones developed. Besides the Emperor, King, Humboldt, and Chinstrap species, the newer species of Adelie, Erect-crested, Fiordland, Galapagos, Gentoo, Little, Macaroni, Royal, Magellanic, Snares, and Yellow-eyed penguins developed. Added to these was the Rockhopper species that arrived from Australinea. As Chief of Chiefs, James lived a nightmare of coping with these species' demands, feeding, and breeding habits. Adding to his problems, he had to handle the continued skirmishes with the Seminoles, many of which were instigated by Penguinist species.

James' most significant challenge was to find a solution to the Meadow of the Olive Tree dispute. The story started one spring morning when every Penguinist and Seminole heard the agonizing voice of Green Majesty. Seminoles noticed that, unlike the earlier times when, after the agonizing voice, the bird flew away, this time, she did not move from her place. The other three birds, upon hearing her, uttered painful shrieks, remaining in their nests, as well. Black Rainbow was sobbing in his place. This happened with the start of a feud between Colonizers and Seminoles over watering the flowers of the Meadow of the Olive Tree. Penguin Colony's Chiefs insisted that since it owned the Pasture, everything on it belonged to Penguin Colony. So, watering the flowers should be its responsibility. The Seminoles responded that Penguin Colony was but a tenant like Lord Marshal, not the Pasture owner. They insisted Seminoles were the real owners and that it was their job to water the flowers. They stated they took turns, sheep, goats, and penguins, watering them for centuries with no dispute arising between them. Neither side was going to make a compromise. The feud continued for days and months. And the shrieks of the Majestic Four Birds only continued and intensified.

James assembled different Penguinists and penguin species, together with Seminole species and guest animals, in a big barn in front of the Meadow of the Olive Tree. He hoped to find a solution to the dilemma of watering the flowers.

He started by saying, "This is our Tree; we planted the root hundreds of years ago!"

A sheep answered him, "How can this be since you have just arrived from Eurainia?"

"He is right, we penguins have planted the tree, and we should water the flowers," answered a Rockhopper Colonizer.

The sheep said, "You, of all penguinists, who do you think you are to talk about this issue? You have no right even to be here! Until a year ago, nobody, not even penguins, knew your species existed! Go back to wherever you came from!"

The Rockhopper answered, "I have more right than you do, sheep; my forefathers waddled on this ranch before any sheep the Creator made."

A Chinstrap Seminole penguin then waddled to the center. As he faced James, he said, "Why do you even raise such an issue? Haven't you heard that we, Seminoles, sheep, goats, and penguins, have always been watering these flowers with no problems? And we will continue to do that; you stay out of it!"

James did not appreciate the tone of the penguin.

At that moment, the Olive Tree branches started withering. Animals present watched with tears and cries. They had never seen the Tree wither before. Soon after, the colorful flowers of the Meadow were turning gray. The animals were in shock!

An Elderly Sheep said, "What we see here is impossible. During the thousands of years of its existence, this Tree has never been in this sad condition. We did not even know it was possible! Look what you have done to it!" He said with a trembling voice.

"Look what you have done!" shouted the Elderly Goats and Chinstraps. James, feeling the heat coming from the Elderly and witnessing the Tree dying, was in awe. He had a puzzled look on his face.

James looked at the penguin with anger and said, "If only

you were not a penguin…" and left the scene. On his way out of the barn, he instructed a Chief Penguinist from his army, named Hayden, to continue the meeting and report to him any outcomes.

Hayden, a Snare Penguinist, was born to a King and Adelie's parents. He was a Penguinist who had delayed his immersion in the Penguinist Bath for a few days only. This Bath wait did not seem to affect Hayden much. He devoted his energy to Penguinistism and used his shrewd mind and small but sturdy body to execute James' orders. But as Snares were, he was practical. Whenever possible, to reduce others' suffering, he did not hesitate to bend the rules, even for Seminoles.

Hayden had a thick yellow stripe running above his eyes and ending in a dropping plume. He had a grouping of white stripes on his cheeks that turned red whenever he was excited or angry. He continued the meeting with the other animals, monitoring but not taking part.

"This is the symbol of the ranch, and you have turned it into a battleground," said a visiting goose, trying to overcome the shrieks.

A small Gentoo Colonizer waddled to the center of the barn. His voice was loud for a Penguinist of his size. "It is our Tree; our eighth Principle is proof of our deep connection to it!"

A goat standing by the door said, "This is ridiculous. Every animal knows that the root had always been there. And each species, goats, sheep, and penguins, owns but a branch."

Deborah, who was still trying to listen to the sides, got inflamed and said, "What is ridiculous is that you think you have a say in this issue. You should be grateful that we invited you to this meeting. You own nothing here. This Tree is ours alone. Our Tree has returned to us!"

"Who cares whose Tree this is? It is just a tree," said a Yellow-eyed penguin.

The arguments continued for hours, but nothing changed. The Majestic Birds continued to shriek in agony, and the Tree

and its flowerbed continued to wither.

But James could not leave the matter unresolved. Even though he was not moved much by the Majestic Birds' agony, still the Tree's withering bothered him terribly. Days after the meeting, he summoned his Chief Penguinists and Seminole Elderly. They continued arguing. After many hours, they could only agree that each species watered the side that belonged to it. But the Tree's condition did not improve. Then, they decided that each species would bring its fertilizer independent of the other two. Still, there was no improvement.

Each species blamed the others for causing the Meadow of the Olive Tree to wither.

"It is the fertilizers you brought that worsened it. It was better before," said a Royal Penguinist to a sheep.

"No, it was your half-dry Penguinist semi-fertilizer that caused it," answered the sheep.

"Well, at least we have worked hard to produce the half-dry semi fertilizer while you just excrete with no toiling!" answered the Royal Penguinist.

"Our fertilizer has nourished this Tree for centuries; how dare you say these things?" answered another sheep.

The controversy went on. The Tree and its Meadow continued to wither. Penguinists brought in expert penguins, and Seminoles brought in expert bulls. Eurainia, upon hearing of the problem, sent expert goats, while Newfarm sent their best geese. They focused their attention on the Tree's root. And none of them could cure it. And none of them could stop the agonizing shrieks of the Majestic Birds. Soon enough, the whole Animal Globe showed interest in the Olive Tree's well-being and the ongoing conflict there.

Failing to find a cure after many years, each of the three species became overprotective of its side. Any animal's undertaking from one species to even walk near another species' branch was treated as a severe breach of the other species' territorial integrity. Over time, internal conflicts among

Seminoles complicated things even further. Sheep fought with goats. Goats with other goats. Wild Goats against goats. Sheep against Wild Sheep. Wild Sheep against Wild Goats. In short, everybody fought against everybody; all thought they had the right cure for the Olive Tree.

On the penguin side, things were not much better. Internal strife, too, was eating up Penguinists and penguins alike. Each of the sixteen species had an opinion. Then, confrontations happened between both camps, Seminoles and penguin-Penguinists. These fights turned violent in the Pasture and the Strip and in Penguin Colony, Eurainia, and the whole Animal Globe. Hundreds of animals were killed.

Then Elderly goats proposed a closer inspection of the branches instead of the root. The conflicting sides agreed that a neutral animal that was neither a penguin nor a sheep nor a goat from Olivia or Penguin Colony should inspect them.

They called an expert goose from Newfarm. After an inspection, she said, "Look, it is clear from the curve of the penguin branch it reaches deeper in the root than the other two branches. Penguins planted this Tree!"

One sheep answered, "You call yourself an expert? Can't you see the sheep branch is the one that has withered less, and it must reach deeper in the root! Sheep planted it!"

The conflict only intensified. And the whole Animal Globe was split over the question of who planted the Olive Tree!

Goats remembered that their ancestors, Elderly Goats, told them long ago that a source of living water under the Tree supported the root and provided it with life.

One of them said, "The Meadow of the Olive Tree was here before any animal ever lived on the ranch."

He tried to remind the other species of this knowledge. Still, Wild Goats from Newfarm and Greenfield silenced him instantly with their menacing looks.

One of them said, "It belongs to penguins; it always has and always will."

Another old Chinstrap Seminole asked, "Do any of you remember what the Elderly crazy Penguin said? I remember very little; my memory is failing me. I only remember two words—over and beyond."

Unfortunately, nobody was as old as he was. They murmured, "Old fool, he has lost it!"

The Meadow of the Olive Tree continued to wither, and the Five Majesties persisted in their anguish.

The conflict over the Meadow of the Olive Tree was the most complicated, but it was not the only one. Ever since Penguin Colony embarked on digging pools in the Pasture and the Strip to serve as recreational areas for Penguinists, there was always unrest and conflict. Quarrels continuously erupted over them. The most heated ones were between Seminoles and one fussy species of Colonizers, the Gentoo Penguinists, who lived in small, isolated cubicles next to these pools.

The Gentoos were a new species that developed because of the change in diet from krill to fish. Even though they were few, their mere presence in those fields caused friction with the Seminoles. They were the most difficult of all Penguinists. They acted independently from the command of Chief Penguinists. It was as if they had formed their own ranch within the ranch. They were even threatening to kill Penguinists if they tried to move or remove them from their cubicles. They were troublemakers, but because they were Penguinists, Chief Penguinists, always concerned with their safety, spent relentless hours and effort to protect them from Seminole attacks.

Gentoos claimed that the Creator at the beginning of time had given them the fields in the water pools immediate surroundings in the Pasture and the Strip. Seminoles maintained that neither Penguin Colony nor its Colonizers had any right to take their Pasture. Both Chief Penguinists and Gentoos built fences around the pools and the contested Terrains to secure them. They prevented any animal except for those of penguin species from approaching them. In many areas within the Pasture and the Strip, recurrence of such security actions had deliberately cut off Seminole animals from their Terrains and barns. Even the centuries-old cycle of free grazing their former leaders allowed them in springtime was no more permissible or accessible.

Trying to circumvent restrictive mobility measures, Seminoles used a wooden raft they built to cross to their Terrains on the other side of the water pools. The Penguinist army caught and detained them. Other Seminoles launched attacks, planned and organized by William the bull, leader of the Seminole Resistance. Even though he lived in Cedarland, he had enough influence over the Seminoles in Olivia. Likewise, other Seminole Resistance members organized and executed multiple attacks on Gentoos and the Penguinist army, killing a few. The Penguinist army retaliated by attacking and killing Seminole sheep and horses. More of such attacks and counter-attacks continued for many months.

James summoned the Chief Penguinists in his barn and discussed the serious incidents. They decided unanimously to build fences around the Seminole Terrains, confining them, and to build more fences separating the Pasture from the rest of Penguin Colony. Only by using access points and blockades controlled by the PCD could Seminoles pass back and forth. Any Seminole caught trying to use alternative access points was punished severely by Penguinist Chiefs. They confiscated his Terrains and even his barn. They also decided to burn the barn of any Seminole involved in violent actions against any penguin species. With more restrictions came more defiance. With defiance came more cruelty and violent actions from both sides. William and Seminole Resistance targeted the cubicles of Penguinists in the Waterfront and the Mountain. Penguin Colony did the same. They attacked Seminoles in the Pasture, the Strip, and Cedarland. For every Penguinist killed, ten Seminoles were slain. The Chief Penguinists hoped that this punishment would deter Seminoles from further attacking innocent penguins. A time came when nobody could tell who started what violent action. The Seminoles often complained to the United Ranch Council, but to no avail.

"Penguin Colony has the right to defend itself!" That was the usual answer.

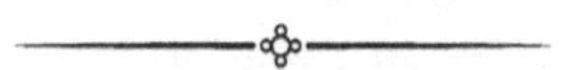

The years passed. Despite the local problems and the continued withering of the Meadow of the Olive Tree, Penguin Colony continued to flourish. The Chief Penguinists moved to live in a newly built White Barn not too far from the Meadow of the Olive Tree. In keeping with the progressive spirit, Old Humboldt had required in the Ten Commandments that Penguin Colony continue electing its Chiefs every four years. After James, they elected Deborah, then Barak, and later Marvin and Isaac. Many penguins from the Animal Globe kept migrating to Penguin Colony.

The continued disruptions to immersion in the Penguinist Bath, the crossbreeding, and the diet change continued to affect Penguinist bodies and minds. Each of the sixteen species elected its own leaders. They followed a different habit of feeding and breeding and had different modes of thinking. There were so many opinions among penguins and Penguinists that challenged the rationale of Chief Penguinists' decision-making. Chief Penguinists longed for the older days of exclusive leadership like Old Humboldt's.

To counter those opinions, Chief Penguinists developed an ingenious strategy of penguin unity. They kept using it one generation after another to keep penguins united. They based it on the fact that penguins pressed together when confronted with danger. At every opportunity, they reminded penguins of the dangers looming over their Penguin Colony. They wrote slogans everywhere.

"We are surrounded by enemies,"

"We must always be united,"

"We should never falter in defending our ranch," and

"Always support your leaders."

Chief Penguinists made special yearly commemoration days for the slaughtered penguins during Mr. Caesar's lunacy. On the commemoration day of Old Humboldt's death, Chief Penguinists reminded penguins of the fire-knackers. Any minor attack by William and the Resistance was inflated and portrayed as a battle for survival. If time passed and there were no such enemy attacks, the leaders made sure they provoked one. They instilled great fear in penguins and Penguinists. Ghandi, with his hawks, made sure that such existential threats reached Eurainia and Newfarm.

Penguins remembered the promises of a "life without fear for penguins in their own ranch" as one of the Penguin Ranch's prime constituents. They remembered the words of their Penguinist hymn, "Penguins of the east, penguins of the west, we will have a life, free from any strife, in our Ranch, we will create, once in the Penguin Ranch." They thought that the continued attacks from the Seminoles and the surrounding ranches and the continued existential threats their leaders have been portraying to them were hardly a fulfillment of that promise!

Add to that, the reawakening experiences, the Colonizers' attitudes and ways of conduct and life, the Seminole Resistance, and many other reasons raised many troubling and vital questions among many penguins and Penguinists.

Many returned to their original homeland in Eurainia, which had become more peaceful and safer for animals.

"Certainly, penguins have been assimilated there now!" they thought.

CHAPTER FOURTEEN

TOWARDS A SOLUTION

One day, on a brisk winter morning, in the Ranch of Egofield, William, the Seminole bull of the Resistance, was sitting in his barn reflecting on the life of Seminoles. He was contemplating the case of Durra, a young lamb and his father on their way to their barn. They were caught by an ongoing violent fight between the Penguinist army and the Seminole Resistance. They both died from knife-beaks while the father tried to protect his lamb's life, using his own slim body as a shield. The Penguinists were trying to defend themselves in their usual violent manner from a Resistance Seminole attack nearby.

William was so caught up in deep thought that he did not notice a pigeon standing on the porch near his window calling his name.

"William, William," the pigeon called and knocked with his beak on the glass window near his stall.

"William."

Finally, William noticed him. He sprang up, opened the window, and let him in.

"Oh, I am sorry, pigeon, I was deep in thought and hardly noticed you," he said with a cautious smile.

"Well, I have sad news for you. Penguin Colony has imposed new rules that confine Seminoles," said the pigeon in a sad tone.

"In the Pasture and the Strip, the number of Seminoles allowed to work has diminished. Penguinists have started confining Seminoles to their Terrains and are restricting their movement heavily."

Alarmed and disappointed, William said, "I am not surprised; it was a matter of time. Penguin Colony Chiefs have always been covetous of our Olivia. They want it as their exclusive property! Their hatred for Seminoles is increasing at an alarming rate!"

The pigeon asked, "What do you want to do, William?"

Saddened by the news, William looked puzzled. The pigeon watched intently and thought he saw tears in his eyes.

William said, "Seminoles do not deserve this treatment; we have been treated unjustly for so long. Animals of the Globe and Penguin Colony are unwilling to let us be who we are. We are a special group of animals, with a deep attachment to our land similar to, maybe more than that of other animals. We want what they want, a normal life."

At this moment, William turned away. He seemed distant, as if in a different world.

William cried out, "What is wrong with the Animal Globe? Can't they see our suffering? Is it our mistake that we were born Seminoles?" His agonizing tone became even higher, "We work very hard under heavy restrictions. It is our sacrifice that made Penguin Colony prosperous, and this is how they repay us!"

William, angry, walked around his stall. His hooves were knocking everything in their way.

He was so furious that the pigeon had to yell out, "William, William, are you alright? Calm down, my friend."

Coming back to reality, William said, "No matter what we do, Penguinists will always look down on us. We will always be guilty of our mere existence! We can never assimilate with Penguinists if they hate us this way. Tell the Chief Bulls in the Midlands that I want to meet them soon."

The pigeon flew to the four corners of the Midlands. After

a short while, William convened a meeting in one of the Midlands barns.

The issue at hand concerned the future of Seminoles and many Midlands ranches that were still licking their wounds from their quick defeat in the last battle with Penguin Colony. Many ranch owners attended the meeting. The Chiefs invited pigeons, sheep, and goats from different ranches. As for William, he invited members and representatives of the Resistance.

When animals assembled and settled, the defiant William marched to the central podium, cleared his throat, and said,

"Olivia was the birthplace of Seminoles. On it, they lived and developed their uniqueness among all of creation in their connection to their land and interconnectedness with each other. Seminoles could grapple with and prevail over cycles of vicious, covetous, and cruel owners and tenants through their steadfast and unfolding will.

"When Animal Globe was still trying to understand why the global droughts and their WARs happened, and when it sought to give justice to species affected by them, regional and global interests sanctioned the Seminole injustice. So, we conclude that justice alone cannot form a fair basis for the cycle of animal history.

"To close the one wound, the Animal Globe opened another. Seminoles had to go through not only one but two existential tragedies: the denial of our existence and the denial of our right to exist as free animals.

"They forced us out of our ranch and forced us to live under unsuitable and horrible conditions for many years. But we never lost our connection and yearning to reestablish ourselves as free animals in our ancient homeland, Olivia.

"They tried everything to test our resilience and hoped that we would forget our Olivia over the years. But contrary to what they expected, we prevailed, and Olivia still lives in our minds and hearts. We kept its memory ever alive. We preserved our language and our Seminole heritage. We have also kept good relations with

our neighbors.

"Our forefathers proclaimed our right to a ranch of our own. After the death of Mr. Otto, Lord Marshal recognized Seminoles as owners of Olivia. The United Ranches Council recognized the Seminoles' past connection to Olivia and confirmed our right to proclaim it as our independent ranch. It required its animals to take steps to achieve that end. From here, I confirm that this recognition by the United Ranch Council of Seminoles' right to establish their ranch is permanent and irreversible.

"Accordingly, we representatives of the Seminoles of Olivia, the Dispossessed Seminoles, and Seminole Migrants around the Globe declare the Independent Ranch of Olivia to be called New Olivia in the Pasture and the Strip. Let animals know that the Meadow of the Olive Tree will be our exclusive property, as it has always been.

"In pursuing our future path, and in accordance with the requirements of progressive global habitat, we acknowledge and ratify any agreement that respects the lives of animals on the Globe. As such, we acknowledge Penguin Colony's right to exist, and we renounce violence and violent action to achieve our freedom."

Animals present, notably those who had known what William had to say, welcomed the announcement. They started barking, humming, bloating, quacking, braying, and neighing with joy and excitement.

Other ranch owners and animals from ranches on good terms with Penguin Colony only pretended to be content. Deep inside, they regretted even attending the meeting. They knew that Penguin Colony would not welcome this announcement. Their presence in that meeting could jeopardize their relationship with it.

Still, groups of the Resistance denounced the announcement. They saw that William had gone over and beyond the limits of any gesture of goodwill towards Penguin Colony. The

Resistance, which William led for many years, was furious.

A horse, a member of the Resistance, said, "Have you lost your mind, William? You know only too well from experience that Penguin Colony only understands one language: fear through violent resistance."

They refused to relinquish the belief that Seminole ownership over three-quarters of Olivia was just and right!

William answered, "Can't you see what is happening? Penguin Colony is a reality! It is here to stay. It is strong, organized, and backed by the most powerful ranches and animals on the Globe. We can keep fighting, but for how long? And what can we achieve?"

Another horse asked, "What about justice? They took away everything from us."

William answered, "After the fire-knackers of Mr. Caesar, the United Ranch Council has redefined the word's meaning. It only applies to Penguins. We do not count, and justice is dead! We must find an alternative way, a way that will compel their attention. We must reawaken the dormant creature and hold it accountable for the very reason of its creation, peace and security to animals. This is the only way. Newfarm requires this as a precondition to hear our cause, and they run the Globe!"

A Wild Sheep, concerned for the Dispossessed Seminoles, asked, "What about the Dispossessed? They are still waiting to return to their barns and Terrains that Penguin Colony took from them by force."

William answered, "I am a Dispossessed myself… let us get their attention first, and I promise you I will defend their case emphatically."

The meeting ended with mixed feelings.

Isaac, the Chief Penguinist of Penguin Colony, upon hearing about the announcement, was furious.

After assembling his Chief Penguinists in the White Barn, he asked them, "Who does this William think he is? How dare he claim that one-third of our ranch belongs to Seminoles?

We must stop him at once. Deborah, I want you to use your connections in Newfarm and Eurainia to stop this ranch from becoming a reality. You, Moses and Ghandi, instruct Penguinists around the Globe to denounce this announcement. They must convey to animals that they cannot allow the birth of another Mr. Caesar in the Midlands. We must stop William before penguins walk the path!"

Still, Isaac felt he needed to do more. He secretly summoned the Colonizers: the Gentoo, Little, and Royal Penguinists and instructed them, "Dig more water ponds in the Pasture and the Strip."

Isaac thought that smaller ponds would not arouse the suspicion of the Globe that he was behind them.

He continued, "Dig them in so many areas of those fields that they ultimately impair Seminoles' movement! I will divert the attention of Penguinists and will instruct the Penguinist army to protect you while you do that."

The three species welcomed the orders with much enthusiasm. After all, this was what they wanted. Having the support of the Chief of Chiefs was beyond their expectation!

Ranches, especially in Eurainia, could not, as much as they wanted to, recognize New Olivia. Chief Bulls had to consider the honey they desperately needed for their feed mixing that Penguin Colony supplied. It involved many Chiefs' interests in the High Tower in the Waterfront. They did not want to jeopardize its security. They were afraid that Isaac and his Chief Penguinists might be right and that they were creating another Mr. Caesar in William. They assuredly did not want to carry the guilt again, sending penguins to the fire-knackers!

Many Chief Bulls in Eurainia kept their feelings ambiguous enough that nobody understood where they stood on the issue. When asked, they dismissed the topic and said,

"It is not up to us; we are bystanders here," or

"It is up to the conflicting sides to decide their future," or

"Every animal can aspire to whatever he wants."

Newfarm's Chiefs welcomed William's approach but did little to move ahead. In the meantime, more ponds were dug in the Pasture. And the tragedy of the Seminoles continued apace. The Olive Tree continued to wither, and the Five Majesties Birds continued to fly and shed colorful feathers with shrieks of pain. When they were settled on the Tree, they continued in their agony.

A year later, the winds of fortune changed direction when Penguinists elected Hayden, the clever, practical, and compassionate Snare Penguinist to succeed Isaac. Of course, being a Penguinist, he continued leading Penguin Colony using the Ten Commandments' directives and spirit. But being a Snare penguin, he saw an opportunity looming for every animal. The New Olivia and Penguin Colony animals noticed that the Five Majesties had stopped their sobbing and painful shrieks.

One Sunday morning, Hayden, Chief of Chiefs in Penguin Colony, assembled the Chief Penguinists to a White Barn meeting. He wanted to discuss the best way to negotiate with Seminoles following William's long-awaited decision to recognize Penguin Colony. As they arrived, Hayden looked at them, one by one. He saw penguins of sorts, shapes, and features.

He thought to himself, "My task will not be easy to convince these penguins of a change of direction!"

Just then, Green and Black Majesty appeared in the skies and flew in circles around the White Barn. Everybody rushed out to look at them. Everybody enjoyed seeing them flying and purring with joy. It was such a rare scene. Seminoles in the Pasture saw them too.

The older bulls said, "We have seen nothing like this! They normally purr in their places, but this is the first time we see them flying and purring. What a joy; we wonder what is going on."

It was so pleasing to hear their purrs instead of their painful shrieks. Upon seeing them, Hayden regained his courage

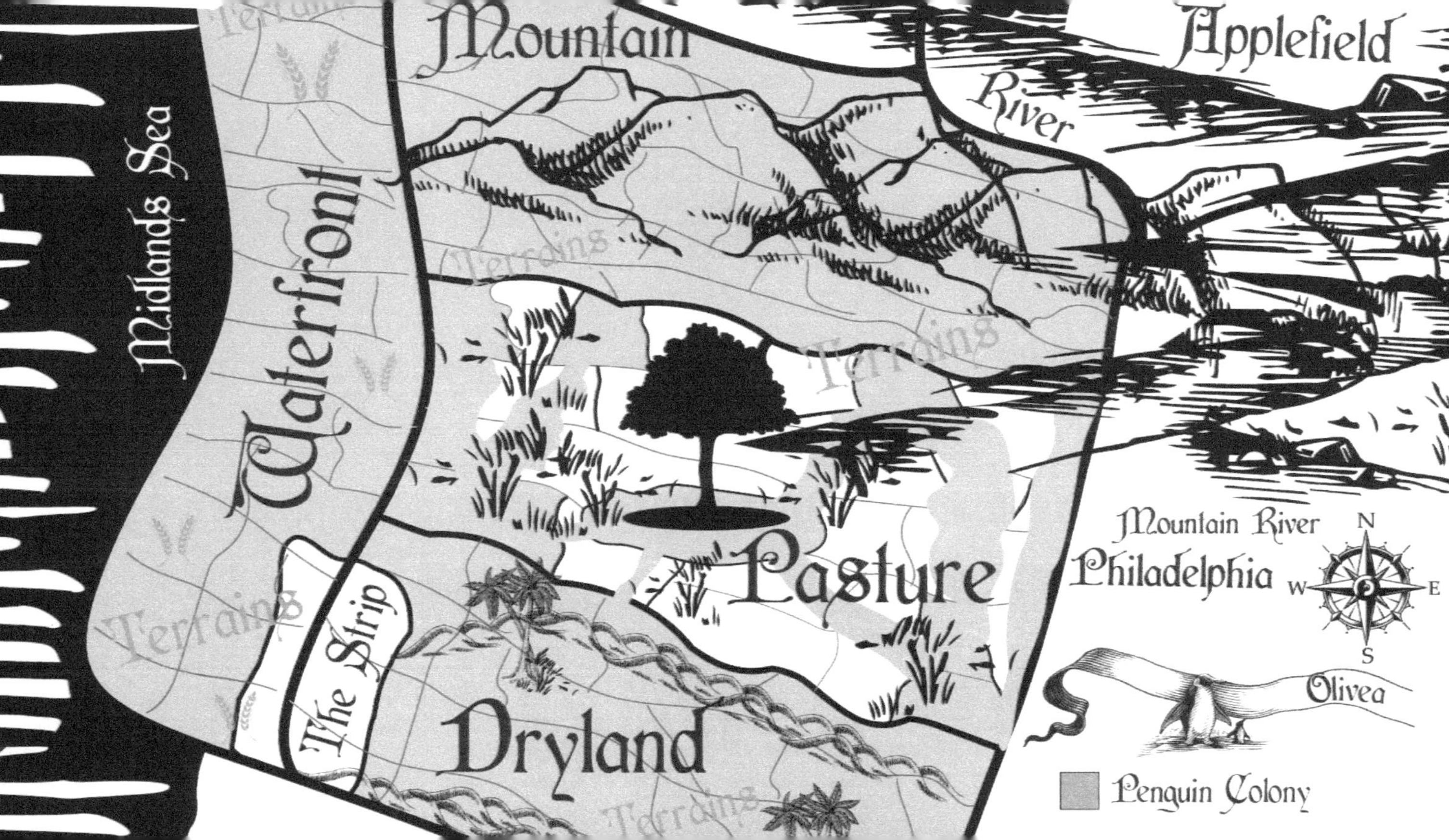

Applefield
Mountain
River
Midlands Sea
Waterfront
Terrains
The Strip
Dryland
Pasture
Mountain River
Philadelphia
Olivea
N E S W
Penguin Colony

and felt that he could sway his listeners' opinions towards his approach.

As penguins resettled in their places, he said, "William, the Seminole Chief, has made a far-reaching compromise. He gave up the Seminole right to the Waterfront, the Mountain, and the Dryland. He is inclined to reconcile with Penguin Colony if we return the Pasture and the Strip to the Seminoles to become their New Olivia ranch."

Humming and nodding filled the White Barn. It was not clear whether they were of joy or of resentment. Many lively discussions happened, while others had a lofty tone and sounded more grumbling than conversing.

"Isn't this what we have been waiting for? We have an opportunity, and we should grab it to have a genuine peaceful Penguin Colony; if not for us, then for our future generations."

He asked for silence again.

"We have suffered enough, and so have the Seminoles. We have been fighting for decades. What have we achieved? Our Penguin Colony is thriving; our fields produce plenty of feed for export, we own a tremendous supply of fish and krill, the Tower we built is twice its standard height, our army is the strongest in the whole region, and we have friends everywhere, but we do not have friends among our immediate neighbors. We do not have peace!

"Our chicks are waddling with fear lest they will be attacked by surprise by a Seminole sheep, goat, or horse. How long? If there is a leader among the Seminoles who we can trust to bring his fellow animals to peace with us, it is William. He is fit for this task!"

Isaac and Marvin interrupted Hayden's speech. They said, "How can you trust this conniving bull? He has been conspiring against us and killing our chicks for a long time!"

Hayden's thick yellow stripe running above his eyes turned more yellow, and his facial plumes pushed upwards. The white stripes on his cheeks turned deep red with anger, and he said,

"Have you forgotten your own history, my friends? How dare you? Don't you remember your role in the battles for the creation of our Penguin Colony? You changed, didn't you? You became Chief of Chiefs despite your atrocious actions. And so has he! He changed just like you!"

At that moment, the remaining Majestic Birds, Red and White Majesty, joined the other two. They flew in circles and purred with joy and excitement. Marvin was astounded, not only by seeing the Birds through the windows but also by that unexpected severe reprimand. He always thought he was doing the right thing for Penguin Colony! But that strident answer made a powerful impression on him. It was as if his entire life flashed in front of him.

He thought, "Could I have been wrong!" He kept silent. As for Isaac, unable to handle the embarrassment, he left the barn.

Then Hayden said, "We are living a glorious lie of our own making. We have been fooling ourselves, thinking that the Seminoles would forget their Olivia as time passed. Well, they have not, and neither have we forgotten our suffering and maltreatment from those who hated us. We wanted freedom, and now we have it! However, to preserve our freedom, we block the freedom of others. Penguins and Seminoles share suffering. Now is the time, dear Penguinists, to assume the role of genuine penguins. It is time to rise above our differences. We must unite under the Penguinist flag and look forward rather than backward. It is time to look for a glorious future and forget a sorrowful past."

He took a deep breath and, with passion, said, "I am going to meet William and try to build a better future for penguins and Seminoles!"

A tremendous commotion started as he said these words. The attendants yelled simultaneously in favor and against the meeting.

Some Penguinists said, "You can't be serious."

"This is absurd."

Others yelled, "The Seminoles are not suffering because of us. We are suffering because of them!"

Still others: "We were here before they were!"

"We give them work on our ranch, and they plot to kill us. We cannot trust Seminoles."

"How can we be safe if we give them control over the Pasture?"

"Are you thinking of giving them our Meadow of the Olive Tree?"

And others yelled back at them, "He is right. William's intentions are genuine!"

"Hayden is a leader with a real vision for the future!"

"Peace is safety for all animal species!"

"The Meadow is not ours or theirs. It is for all animals!"

The heated arguments calmed only after Hayden started singing the Penguinist hymn.

Penguins of the east, penguins of the west, penguins, penguins all over the Globe, rejoice, rejoice, rejoice.

Our hope is alive, as ever as it was; a ranch of our own, hundreds of years alive, penguins, penguins all over the Globe.

Penguins of the east, we pledge to work hard, Penguins of the west, we pledge not to give up the right, the right above every other right.

Penguins of the east, penguins of the west, we will have a life, free from any strife, in our own ranch, we will create, once in the penguin ranch.

Great shall be the world we sow, for all the animals on the Globe, they will achieve even more, for our success is the success of them all.

Penguins of the east, penguins of the west, rejoice, rejoice, rejoice."

The words of the hymn echoed in many souls. They felt a

better understanding of his speech. Repeating Hayden's words in their hearts and minds, they still saw his commitment to the Penguinists and the penguin cause. It differed from everything they had heard before in their lives, but it was captivating enough to change their hearts and minds. They wanted a life with no strife on their ranch, and they gave him the support he needed. But others were not as convinced.

It took him two months of tough negotiations to get the majority to organize a meaningful meeting with William. Hayden conveyed his intentions to the leaders of Eurainia and Newfarm. They liked and embraced the idea. Newfarm's Chief of Chiefs, Mr. Felton, invited both leaders to Newfarm for the talks.

William knew the negotiations over the Dispossessed Seminoles' return and the Meadow of the Olive Tree would be challenging. He told Mr. Felton during a preparatory meeting, "I am not sure whether Chief Hayden is ready to acknowledge the Seminole right of return to our Terrains and our rightful ownership of the Meadow! I am not even sure that he acknowledges our New Olivia as a ranch. I believe that, given the circumstances, all we can achieve is to begin the talks. As the leader of the Globe's most progressive ranch, I do not think that your presence, Mr. Felton, is necessary at this stage! If negotiations fail, as they are bound to, you as host will look for someone to blame. And since I am the weaker side in this, and you have a unique relationship with Hayden and Penguin Colony, your finger will naturally point at me!"

Mr. Felton, from his side, was facing severe challenges to his rule from Newfarm's animals. He needed to show his animals that he could still do good and that he was still fit to lead them. Mr. Felton, therefore, promised William, "Chief William, I promise to do my best to support your case with Hayden, and if negotiations fail, I will not blame you!"

He convinced William, who thought that with Mr. Felton on his side, he could tilt the balance to the Seminoles' justified cause and resolve the issues at hand.

The day of the meeting came. Many Chief Penguins and Penguinists, and many bulls, rams, goats, and sheep from all over the Animal Globe attended it. Dozens of pigeons and hawks were also present. All were excited to see two enemies embrace, signaling a fresh beginning. The two leaders talked about rosy pictures of their respective ranches once they completed the agreement. They met for some time regularly and gained each other's trust despite their differences.

During the talks, something strange was happening to the Meadow of the Olive Tree. A bright white cloud appeared in the skies right over the Olive Tree. The Olive Tree came back to life, and the four Majestic Birds continued purring. Contrary to his usual habit of expressing his joy in situ, the fifth Bird, Black Rainbow, flew from one Majestic Bird to another. He seemed as if he was talking to them. Then he disappeared into the white cloud above and came down again. He flew joyfully over the animals gathered at the Meadow of the Olive Tree, and the three main animal species were overjoyed to see him flying that way. Then he returned to the Tree and resettled in the center. It was a magnificent scene, and everybody noticed it!

No animal was competent or knowledgeable enough to understand who these Birds were and why they reacted so.

After a few days of negotiations, both Seminole and Penguin Colony pigeons reported that an agreement was imminent.

These reporting birds were more excited over the meeting's potential outcomes than the reality. As William expected, the two leaders faced a significant problem. Both of them contested each other's claim to ownership of the Meadow of the Olive Tree. They, likewise, had opposing views of what "the right of the Dispossessed to return" to their Terrains meant. They turned to their host, Mr. Felton, Newfarm's Chief of Chiefs, for a solution.

Mr. Felton, intending to pressure both sides, said, "I want to be truthful with you. I know little about the Meadow of the Olive Tree or to whom it belongs. Still, I can promise you this:

I cannot risk my reputation as Chief of Chiefs of the Animal Globe's leading ranch for a futile talk! Both of you find a solution!"

But the two leaders could not.

In the meantime, hawks reported to the Penguinists in Penguin Colony that Hayden was making concessions. They reported that Hayden would recognize the ranch of New Olivia and might return ponds within the Pasture back to the Seminoles. They also reported that he was conceding the Meadow of the Olive Tree over to the Seminoles. The Gentoo and Little Penguinists protested in front of his White Barn at the Waterfront in Penguin Colony. They threatened to use violence if any such news were correct.

The situation in the Pasture and the Strip was not different. Pigeons reported William too was conceding to Hayden Pasture Terrains and even the Meadow of the Olive Tree. Threats of violence were being heard there.

Mr. Felton was aware of these developments through his eagles living on the Tower of the Waterfront. Hayden's well-being concerned him especially.

He said to William, "I investigated the issue extensively and have concluded that the Meadow of the Olive Tree belongs to Penguin Colony. However, in return for your recognition, Hayden will commit to allowing dozens of Seminoles to return to Penguin Colony."

William was furious with the Chief's conclusion.

He said to him, "Dozens, only dozens! The Penguinists expelled thousands from their homes! I agreed to work fully with you according to your promises. What you are asking me is not what you promised! No Seminole will ever accept this!"

The Chief answered, "This is how it will be, and you have to accept it!"

William moved back and forth, sniffing deeply at the white hair covering his eyes.

He answered, "If I accept this, I invite you to my funeral

tomorrow, Mr. Felton!"

"If you do not accept this, you are not fit to lead the Seminoles!" answered Mr. Felton.

The negotiations collapsed. Everybody returned to their Terrains. And Mr. Felton blamed William for the failure!

Back in Penguin Colony, Hayden tried hard to convince Penguinists that what they heard was not correct! But some refused to believe him. A zealous Gentoo Penguinist attacked Hayden, calling him a "traitor," and slit his throat. He was staunchly opposed to any meetings with William and any concessions to Seminoles.

Some Seminole Wild Sheep opposed to the meetings also attacked innocent Penguinists in Penguin Colony, killing many. Then the Penguinist army retaliated with extreme force, killing many Seminoles. This action-reaction continued for months. There was fear all over Penguin Colony. When the next elections came, the fearful Penguinists elected Nathan, a potent King Penguinist well known for his relentless concern for Penguin Colony's safety, to lead them.

Nathan launched massive-scale operations to punish the Seminoles for their violent action. He made it his aim to destroy everything Hayden worked for. Nathan stopped the meetings with William and declared him an enemy of Penguin Colony.

When a pigeon asked why he stopped the meetings, he answered, "It is a waste of time. The Seminoles and William are treacherous, and we cannot trust them. They are after the destruction of our Penguin Colony. This is not a time for talks. It is time for survival! We have to press together and defend ourselves!"

Two months later, Nathan ordered his Penguinist army to besiege William's barn. During the siege, William became sick with a mysterious disease and died two months later. An expert goose from Rhonefield, who checked his body, declared that he had died of a rare poison. But nobody could pinpoint the culprit. The Seminoles, sad and dismayed, buried him as a hero.

Thousands of Seminoles attended his solemn funeral.

Adjacent to his barn, his successor Chief constructed a unique rectangular plaza at the center of which stood William's tomb. The plaza itself was decorated with bundles of colorful flowers arranged in a rectangle around the tomb. Three Seminole flags stood diagonally on each corner. The tomb itself was decorated with a drawing of Olivia's Olive Tree. On his tombstone, Seminoles wrote, "Here lies William, who spent all his life trying to return Olivia to its rightful owners. He is the hero, the father, and the symbol of Olivia."

William's Tomb Plaza

The Seminoles elected a bull called Aram to succeed William as Chief. Aram tried his best to keep the Seminole cause alive, but he certainly lacked William's charisma. And indeed, Penguin Colony was adamant about keeping him and all the Seminoles subordinate to its power and control.

Every year, Seminoles held a special ceremony to honor William and generations of Seminoles who lost their lives in the service of Olivia. During the ceremony, two horses, eight sheep, and two goats, each carrying a pole with a Seminole flag, marched around the tomb three times before placing the flags in their proper places.

Soon after William's death, the four White Majestic Birds settled on the Olive Tree, Black Majesty, White Majesty, Red Majesty, and Green Majesty flew with excruciating and piercing cries. They flew around the Meadow three times. Before they disappeared on the horizon, they shed their colored feathers over the Meadow. After that, no animal has seen them on the ranch!

Black Rainbow, the Bird with a rainbow tail, saw the in-chorus disappearance of the Four Majesties. He cried and sighed for a few days. His cries suggested he was calling for them, but the four Majesties never returned. His rainbow tail lost its shine. Finally, he gave up and breathed his last.

The bright cloud that overshadowed the Meadow of the Olive Tree disappeared, and the Olive Tree and its Meadow started to wither again!

PART FOUR

CHAPTER FIFTEEN

RECURRENCES

Black Majesty appeared in the skies of one ranch in Olympia. She appeared sobbing and shedding a trail of Black feathers over the heads of a multiplicity of animal species fleeing from the ranch to the ranch's borders. These refugees soon organized themselves into a unified group under the leadership of a Chief Bull called Kaaga.

Kaaga organized and trained dogs and goats to become an army of killers. He led various attacks on the mother ranch, intending to overthrow its Chief of Chiefs. The Chief of Chiefs rallied his army of dogs against Kaaga. They exchanged accusations and battles over many years, killing many animals on both sides. Throughout the conflict, the Four Majestic Birds continued appearing in the skies individually or in pairs over different times.

Kaaga and the Chief of Chiefs found a solution to their problems by sharing leadership. Many animals from both camps opposed the agreement and tried to topple it using force and violence. The worst attempt came when animals from the Chief of Chief's camp sought to exterminate their opponents, their "final solution" to an agreement they opposed. The four Majestic Birds appeared in the skies with endless shrieks. Their colored feathers left an endless trail on the soil, washed in the blood of thousands of innocent animals butchered for no reason other than belonging to Kaaga's group or supporting the peaceful solution. The butchering continued for one hundred days. It stopped after Kaaga sent another fierce army of dogs to face and kill the opponents. As this conflict ended, another one started in an adjacent ranch, with reasons connected to the first one. The cycle of violence continued for years.

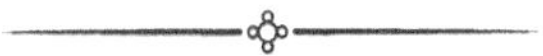

Nigerland was a ranch on the western side of Olympia. The ranch's population comprised goats and sheep, hens, ducks, and pigeons. They lived in relative harmony for many years until a Wild Sheep group called Boko's Group changed everything. This group maintained that sheep were a superior species over the rest of the animals. They despised and antagonized animal species that did not believe in what Wild Sheep believed. This meant that their wrath could turn against other sheep over any disagreement. For them, the truth about sheep's superiority came from their book—which, according to them, other sheep misunderstood. Their interpretation of the book required Wild Sheep to coerce other animal species into accepting *their* truthful teachings. According to Wild Sheep, "We are saving your species from *eternal damnation*."

So, they were to fight any species that rejected their teachings until it was either killed or saved!

Many sheep lived in the northern part of the ranch, while most goats lived in the southern part—both species used to visit both parts with no harassment. One day, the Wild Sheep started engaging other sheep in a conversion conversation. Not moved by any arguments presented, some went their way. Others joined their ranks after Wild Sheep revealed to them the book's hidden parts of endless rewards. Boko's Group increased in number. Then they turned their attention to the other species, intending to save them, of course! When the goats rejected their claims, they were furious, and their teachings turned into a bloodbath of goats. Pigeons narrated the events to the goats living in the south, who rallied their forces and attacked Boko's Wild Sheep, causing a bloodbath of sheep. Thousands of animals died. Neighboring ranches joined the fights, taking sides. In no time, the whole ranch watched the worst massacres since the droughts and the WARs. The Four Majestic Birds kept showing up, individually or in a group, in the skies of the ranch, shedding their wet feathers, but to no avail!

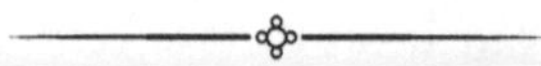

At different times, over many years, the Majestic Four, individually or in a group, appeared in Asiana's skies. Towards the end of the first drought and WAR I, Mr. Pixner of Rhonefield declared himself landlord over a ranch in Asiana called Nam. He continued his unfettered rule until WAR II, when Japaland invaded Nam, claiming legitimate ownership. Newfarm, Redfield, and Eastland, enraged, dispatched their dog armies to support Rhonefield until they ousted Japaland. Before Mr. Pixner could claim victory, however, he found himself entangled in another conflict.

The animals of Nam wanted their independence and rejected him as the landlord. His dogs fought Nam's dogs, and gruesome, bloody times continued. Every day, they killed dozens of fighting dogs from both sides. In no time, the powerful ranches on the Globe changed the rules of conflict. Redfield and its ally Eastland supported the northern part of Nam. They declared its independence, while Newfarm and its ally Australinea supported the ranch's southern part and declared its independence.

Dog armies from the north, who were from the same species as the south's dogs, infiltrated the south and caused domestic clashes. This extended for years. Newfarm had to send its dogs to protect the innocent animals caught in the battles. The fighting killed thousands of Newfarm's dogs but more of Nam's animals from both north and south species. In one battle, battered dogs from both north and south concluded that neither side would win. They agreed to work out their differences by uniting north and south and ousting Newfarm's dogs from further intervention.

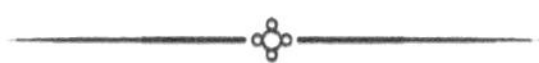

When Mr. Otto was young, he commanded a large army of dogs. He had expanded his rule to various ranches around the Animal Globe. The ranch of Yuguslave in eastern Eurainia was under his rule for many years. Six different Terrains and animals of varied species lived on it. Some Terrains had more of one species than another. His actions of favoritism toward one animal species over another, such as Pramenka sheep over goats, and Tauernsheck goats over Poitou goats, had created an arrangement of volatile unity between the animals.

In Yuguslave's center, a Terrain had a mix of sheep and two goat species. When Mr. Otto died, each of the six Terrains decided they wanted independence. They wanted to divide Yuguslave based on species ownership of land. A controversy arose between the animals regarding how to do that since Terrains had mixed goat and sheep species. In no time, a bloody conflict arose between the different species. It started when the sheep first declared their independence in one Terrain. Both goat species, opposing that independence, rammed the sheep with extensive cruelty, killing many of them. They attacked because they refused to have so many goats living in the same Terrain under sheep rule. The sheep retaliated with even more cruelty. One Terrain after another within the ranch got involved in fighting, leading to the killing of thousands of animals. Then, the conflict spread to neighboring ranches, and this continued for years. The Four Majesties appeared in the skies of the Terrains and the ranches. They flew together, but most of the time, they flew in pairs. During the years, the fighting animals always disregarded their agonizing cries and wet feathers that increased exponentially. In the end, the parties reached a resolution when they declared each Terrain an independent ranch.

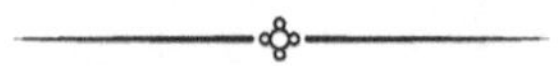

In the southern part of the Midlands, in the ranch of Yemini, lived two species of sheep, the Awassi sheep and the Arabi sheep breeds. For many years, the two species got along well because they feared their Chief of Chief's retaliation with his massive army of dogs. Inspired by the decisive rebellious actions of the animals of neighboring ranches, who ousted their brutal leaders, the Arabi sheep tried a similar approach to oust their leader. They stopped working in their Chief's fields and demanded his resignation.

The Awassi sheep refused to let him go because he gave them lots of feed rations. So, they turned against the Arabi sheep species. The Chief of Chiefs sent his dogs after the Arabi sheep, supported by the Awassi sheep. Battles ensued for months, and they killed thousands of sheep. The continued pressure from the United Ranch Council and neighboring ranches convinced the Chief to resign.

The Yemini animals elected an Arabi sheep as the new Chief of Chiefs. But the former Chief never lost his appetite to return to his earlier power and rule. In his mind, "If I am not ruling, then let them kill each other!" He incited and aroused the Awassi sheep, causing instability against the elected Arabi sheep's rule. Neighbor ranches got involved, taking sides and sending armies of dogs and sheep to fight. The battles progressed for years, and thousands of animals lost their lives, even more so because of starvation and disease. All that time, the Four Majestic Birds appeared in the skies of the ranches involved. As the animals disregarded them, their trail of wet, colored feathers covered the land.

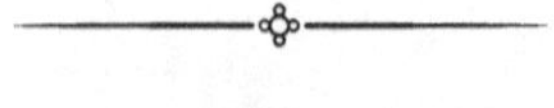

Crimes were being committed in one locality on the Globe while other battles were happening elsewhere. The Four Majesties flew frantically from one place to another until their wings could no longer carry their body weight. The heavy pain that they carried from every crime committed and every animal wasted intensified their wails. Many of the massacres mounted in comparable severity and significance to Mr. Caesar's penguin fire-knackers.

The recurrent transgressions impeded the Four Majestic Birds from returning to their nests in the Meadow of the Olive Tree in New Olivia.

CHAPTER SIXTEEN

RESURGENCE: MORE RECURRENCES

The years passed. One day in early spring, on a clear Sunday morning with a fine blue sky, during the Seminole and Penguinist daily squabble over whose right it was to water the flowers of the Meadow of the Olive Tree, a young goat noticed movement on top of the Olive Tree. He stood on a small hill opposite the Meadow, watching the argument from a distance.

"Everybody, be silent!" he yelled.

"Who are you to ask us for silence?" said a Penguinist.

"Just be silent and come and see! Something is happening above your heads; come and see!"

The young goat looked so bewildered and terrified that the animals arguing were silenced. The young goat became more baffled. The animals ran towards him. As they turned and looked up, they saw a white cloud above the Olive Tree. The cloud's appearance was strange because it was such a clear day.

"Where did this cloud come from?" asked a sheep.

The animals fell to the ground when they saw a dazzling bright light coming from the cloud over the Olive Tree. The light shined on them, and nobody could look up. Terrified, they looked at each other.

"Oh no, what is going on?" they cried out.

Then, they saw different colors reflecting on their bodies as the brightness diminished. Looking up, they saw something they thought could never happen. A rainbow light came from the cloud, covering the whole tree and adorning every wrinkled leaf with bright, dazzling colors.

Black Rainbow, whom the animals had presumed dead for many years, moved his head. His dull rainbow tail embraced the rays of colored light coming from the cloud as if unifying his colors with their colors. The animals could not believe what they were witnessing. He lifted his body. The three feathers on his head brightened, and he opened his dimmed eyes.

A goat said, "Look, Black Rainbow! Everybody, look at Black Rainbow; he is moving, he is alive! He is back!"

Everybody watched the extraordinary resurgence.

They said, "How can this be! This is impossible! This is incredible!"

Black Rainbow, who absorbed energy from the rays, stretched his wings. After a few seconds, he flew up and down with great delight. Then he made distinct sounds as he flew from one empty nest to the other of the Four Majestic Birds. In no time, the Majestic Four Birds reappeared in the sky. They flew from the four corners of the ranch and perched in their places. Black Rainbow, now more excited, kept flying from one Majesty to the other. It was clear he was welcoming them back. The cloud and its colored rays disappeared, and the sky cleared again. Everybody was in awe. They kept talking as if there were no decades-long dispute between them. Minutes ago, they were enemies, but that mysterious moment made them friends.

Seminoles who witnessed it rushed back to the main barn and shared with their Chiefs what they saw. Chief Abe, who had replaced William as the Seminole leader, asked for details. The Seminoles explained the events as they happened.

"This is excellent news!" he said. "Since a Seminole goat saw the event first, it is proof that the Meadow of the Olive Tree is ours."

He paused, then said, "Pigeons, go out and tell the Globe that a hero Seminole has witnessed this miracle first. Tell them that this proves our rightful ownership of the Meadow."

The Penguinists shared with their Chief Penguinists what happened.

Nathan, their Chief of Chiefs, said, "I can understand that the Majestic Birds returned to their nests, but you do not have to exaggerate with this unbelievable nonsense."

After thinking for a minute, he said, "Still, this is excellent news; this proves to the Globe that the Meadow of the Olive Tree is ours. Our resilience and persistence in protecting it from Seminoles have paid off, and the Birds have returned to their rightful owner, Penguin Colony."

He paused again and then ordered his hawks, "Go out and announce to the whole Globe that our resilient protection of the Meadow has paid off; we are the rightful owners!"

After a few days, the paradoxical news of the Majestic Four Birds' return to their Meadow spread everywhere.

The headlines read,

"A miracle Seminole goat witnessed
the return of the Majestic Four."
"The Majestic Four return miraculously
because of a Seminole goat."

On the opposite side, the hawks disseminated the news as follows:

"The Majestic Four return
to their homeland in Penguin Colony."
"Resilience paid off, Penguin Colony
reclaims its Majestic Four."

In the details of the announcements, both sides asked for continued support to carry forward the Meadow's cause. Both leaders, and their Chiefs, received acclaim and support.

The perversion of the truth did not satisfy the animals who watched the event. That the most significant event of their entire experience, Black Rainbow's resurgence, was reported by neither side irritated them even more. They shared the details of the miracle with their Elderly, Chinstraps, Goats, and Sheep. These coordinated their efforts and created something they called the Dialogue among the species.

They met in a big barn to converse and present their views of what each group thought had happened. Before the Dialogue meeting started, they promised they would hold the discussions respectfully and without fights.

The Chinstrap penguins presented their remarks. They said, "Whereas miracles happen, the only one is the return of the Four Birds. Black Rainbow was not dead but asleep."

Other animals asked, "Then how can a bird sleep for many years?"

The Elderly Sheep said, "Whereas miracles are possible, Black Rainbow could not have remained on the Tree without the other four. The witnesses flinched and could not see: a bird that looks exactly like Black Rainbow came from the cloud and replaced him."

Other animals answered, "How do you explain then that for ages animals saw his dead body on the Tree? Can so many witnesses flinch, all at the same time?"

The Elderly goats said, "Miracles can happen, and this one is surely a miracle. Black Rainbow was dead and came back to life, and he was the one to call the other Four Birds. It is unmistakable from the account we heard."

Other animals responded, "No animal has ever returned from the dead; there is no way you can prove this!"

The Elderly agreed to disagree. The meeting ended with little progress or understanding of what happened on that tree.

These arguments only intensified among the Elderly over the following days and months in New Olivia and Penguin Colony. The Chiefs of both further developed the arguments of their respective Elderly species. Seminole Chiefs argued for Seminole Elderly and Penguinist Chiefs for Penguin Elderly. They tried to encourage support for their positions in the five Farms of the Animal Globe, Eurainia, Newfarm, Australinea,

Olympia, and Asiana. Some Chief Bulls in the five Farms stood by the Seminole Chiefs and their Elderly animals.

In contrast, others stood by Penguin Colony Chiefs and their Elderly Penguinists. Every Chief adopted the position of one side. The Chiefs then shared their positions with their ranch's Elderly animals. Many Elderly rejected it. For every argument proposed by one Elderly species, another proposed another counterargument. After months, there was no telling who proposed what and why. Everything became a jumble of ideas and positions. It was as if the resurgence event kindled the whole Animal Globe with fire.

The arguments of one species convinced members of another. Goats adopted Penguinist arguments, penguins adopted goat arguments. Sheep adopted goat arguments. Goats adopted sheep arguments. Every one of these took the new arguments and tried to convince their respective species. They convinced a few. In the end, each species split itself. Goats looked like goats but spoke like penguins. Penguins looked like penguins but spoke like sheep. Sheep looked like sheep but spoke like penguins. Animals from all the species found ingenious ways to blend this "miraculous" incident on the Olive Tree with their own views. They combined them with the views presented by the pigeons and hawks.

Intellectually focused geese, who spent their lives studying animals' habitats, also had an opinion upon hearing the news.

They said, "We cannot explain miracles; they are not rational; clouds appear in the sky all the time. So do rainbows. It just happened that they both appeared in the sky at the same time on a particular day. These birds come and go. So what? We know that. There is no connection between the black bird and the white birds. If reason cannot explain it, then it must be wrong! Those who believe in miracles are hallucinating!"

Yet, amid these diverse and opposing opinions, the original witnesses to the resurgence incident never faltered. They were sure that the impossible event they saw was a reality;

it was worth dying for! From that day onwards, their eyes were open to an alternative way of life, to a rejuvenation that moved beyond any species' physical appearance. What united them was not the species they belonged to—goat, sheep, or penguin—but an event that transcended every species: Black Raninbow's resurgence and the Four Majesties' return. They called themselves Resurgents. Resurgents traveled all over the Globe, trying to convince other animals of their beliefs. They wrote a book and developed a way of life based on harmonious coexistence with every animal species and the environment. They swayed many animals; their numbers increased at such a rate that many Chiefs felt alarmed.

Sheep could not believe how sheep could act like Resurgent goats. Penguins could not believe how penguins could imitate Resurgent sheep. Even pigs who despised penguins imitated Resurgent penguins. In no time, the Resurgent movement spread around the Globe. And so did persecution against its adherents. Resurgents became one of the most persecuted groups of animals on the Animal Globe. A Resurgent book was burnt daily, and a barn was destroyed somewhere in the Animal Globe's five Farms. The appearances and shrieks of the four agonizing Majestic Birds continued.

The whole controversy from the beginning intrigued many animals. They were like vampires, feeding and feasting on it. They created slogans of hatred and continued to despise other species who disagreed with them. Soon enough, the hatred picked up a momentum of its own; it became a hatred for the sake of hatred. Its adherents worked for years to develop propaganda material that brainwashed animals' minds with their hidden hate agendas. They found devoted listeners among the younger generations of animals. Lambs, kids, calves, piglets, and young penguins became soldiers of hatred, waiting for a trigger to come out. These confronted and assaulted other species.

Because of an increase in such incidents and the gravity

of their consequences, the United Ranch Council named the phenomena Hate Crimes. The most notorious of hate crimes was Mr. Caesar's hatred of penguins because of their skin color. The Council, with its Assembly determined never to allow such hate to reach those levels ever again, fought against the crimes and punished their culprits. Every ranch on the Globe enacted rules and regulations to fight against what they called *domestic hate crimes.*

Now and again, animals heard of a hate crime happening somewhere on the Globe. Newfarm, which had multiple species of animals, faced an increased level of hate crimes every day. Many of them were directed towards the multi-color but specifically black-colored Angora goats that formed one-tenth of goat species in Newfarm. Black Angora goats lived and worked in Newfarm, planting and harvesting like other goats there. Still, animals from other species, including goats on the ranch, hated and persecuted them for an entrenched reason. During these crimes, one or more of the Majestic Four appeared in the sky, agonizing and leaving a trail of colored feathers. Of course, the perpetrators of hate crimes believed they were fighting for a just cause. According to them, "It is the right thing to do!"

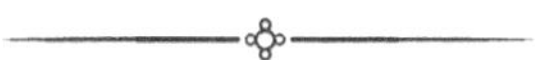

One of the hate crime conflicts had a severe significance and touched the lives of many animals. A group of Wild Sheep from the Midlands started it. The Penguinist victory and the various conflicts and WARs over the years had left a leadership void in a few Midlands ranches. Wild Sheep jumped in to fill that void. Like Boko's group in Nigerland, they justified their violent actions based on their book of teachings. As a result, when their neighbor goats, penguins, Resurgents, and even other sheep rejected their teachings, they let their wild nature out and turned to violent fighting. They had been training their younger lambs in the art of attacking animals, using their bodies with their dense heads and curved horns as a killing tool.

The controversy over the Meadow of the Olive Tree only intensified their wild nature since they were among those sheep that were sure Black Rainbow came out of the cloud. At first, they tried to explain to their neighbors that they were mistaken about the resurgence incident, but their neighbors ignored them. It was in no time they started a massive-scale attack on their opponents. Their curved horns and solid heads rammed thousands of innocent animals of the other species. After taking a couple of ranches in the Midlands under their control, they felt strong enough to attack beyond the Midlands, setting their sights on Eurainia, Olympia, Australinea, and even Newfarm, the strongest ranch of the Animal Globe. Using the cover of night, hundreds of Wild Sheep unanimously rammed into two Towers, symbols of progressive life, in the center of Newfarm. As the Towers collapsed, they killed hundreds of innocent animals. Newfarm's Chief of Chiefs, infuriated, dispatched his dog army against them in the Midlands' ranches. The fights continued for years. They killed many Wild Sheep, and many innocent animals were caught in the fight. One or more of the Four Majesties' regular visits increased during these years, shedding endless wet, colored feathers.

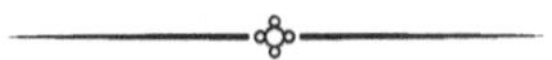

More hate crimes happened on one ranch of Australinea when a group of penguins had their barn door burst open. A Wild Goat equipped with his sharpened horns went from one penguin to another, killing and injuring many. Red Majesty flew over that barn, but the Wild Goat disregarded her, shook her feathers from his body, and barged into that barn. The same thing happened when a group of sheep gathered in another barn, and a Wild Goat barged in and killed many. In Egofield, in the Midlands, dozens of hate crime attacks were perpetrated by Wild Sheep against goats and Resurgents. The Majestic Four Birds appeared and reappeared, but all the time, animals ignored them.

Within each species, a conflict of opinion trapped many animals. Division and resentment became the norm. It was as if animals were just waiting for a reason for hatred, bigotry, and confrontation. Sheep wrestled with other sheep and penguins with other penguins. Sheep collaborated with goats against other sheep. Penguins collaborated with sheep against other penguins. The list was endless. Here, too, the division took on its own impetus, and sometimes it escalated into violent conflict.

Such was the case of the Valdostana goats. They believed that Black Rainbow's resurgence was the end of something great. The Valais BlackNeck goats believed his resurgence was the beginning of something great. As trivial as it was, this difference of opinion created tension between the two species. It culminated in an outright conflict in one of Greenfield's western Terrains when Valais BlackNeck goats decided not to allow Valdostana goats to work the land with them. BlackNeck goats insisted that Lord Marshal should give them the Terrain and that they could do what they wanted with it. As a result, Valdostana goats could not receive their feed rations. Thousands of them died from starvation. The species revolted against Lord Marshal, and the Valais BlackNeck goats demanded independence of their Terrain from him.

Lord Marshal, wanting to make peace between the two goat species, partitioned that Terrain into two, north and south, one for each species. In the northern part, the two goat species lived together, segregated, but still lived side by side. The partition meant that members of each species had to move from their homes to the other side of the partitioned territory. Some from both species supported partition, but many did not. It was only a matter of time before the species fought each other. Hundreds ended up killed, many of whom were innocent bucks and nannies trapped in the wrong place at the wrong time. The Four Majestic Birds often appeared during all these times.

The conflict ended only after Lord Marshal convinced both species that "Black Rainbow's resurgence was the beginning and the end of something great, both at the same time."

Tensions decreased, and both species became more receptive to the needs of the other. They learned to put their minor past differences aside and look forward to a flourishing future.

Still, other animals distanced themselves from the controversy. It became too much to deal with. Their focus on life changed from the global to the narrow, immediate family.

These animals said, "Global concerns are not worth fighting for anymore," or "Our family is more important!" or "Our leaders and our Elderly will do the right thing for us!"

They gave up the right to think of global issues and continued their life with no opinion and a limited purpose. They, too, felt they were doing the right thing.

Upon seeing the problems that the Meadow of the Olive Tree caused to animals' lives, together with atrocities committed because of a belief system, many animals altered their lives altogether. To them, beliefs and the following of a legalistic structure led to an exacerbated ego. Ego, if antagonized, can lead both the assailant and the defender to absolute perdition. Mr. Caesar and his Chief Pigs exemplified the problematic aspects of ego in no uncertain terms. These animals rid themselves of any connection to any belief altogether. They adopted a materialistic, non-mystical approach, a completely intellectually driven approach to life and each other. Neither the Meadow nor the Five Majesties meant anything to them. They thought they were doing the right thing.

Chaos and confusion over meaning and purpose had made animals on the Globe lose connection with their physical identities and inward sentiments. New identities were being born. Former enemies became friends, and best friends became enemies. Feelings, beliefs, and meanings were becoming harder to express and understand. When animals thought they resolved one, another challenge came their way and had made them rethink their conclusions. With or without their knowledge, animals on the Animal Globe became connected to the Meadow of the Olive Tree and the Five Majesties.

Conflicts and WARs became normality to animal life all over the Animal Globe. Adversarial ranches and adversarial species of animals rushed into conflict. In contrast, ranches and animal species that could have prevented the conflict took their time before getting involved. And even when they got involved, their involvement was less based on promoting peace and security and more on careful calculation of enhancing their own welfare and influence.

Amid these global misfortunes, the Meadow of the Olive Tree in New Olivia resumed its tragic withering, and the Majestic Five Birds returned to their animal-caused suffering and agonies.

CHAPTER SEVENTEEN

GLOBAL DISEASE, INVISIBLE ENEMY

Despite the conflicts and WARs in ranches on the Animal Globe, ranch development continued for some ranches. The conditions for animal life improved and progressed, based on experimentation and trial and error. The rivalry continued between the ranches, and each tried to prove its superiority over the others. Rivalry increased between Redfarm and Newfarm, but especially between Newfarm and Eastland. Eastland tried to match, even replace, the superiority and the leadership of Newfarm on the Animal Globe at any potential opportunity. Of course, Newfarm was unwilling to yield its leadership to either Redfarm or Eastland or any other ranch on the Animal Globe. For every advancement that any of them produced, Newfarm maintained that it had produced it before them. If it did not possess the advancement, the Chiefs employed their well-informed geese and most intelligent animals to produce a superior innovation. Redfarm, more so Eastland, did similar actions to continue the cycle of rivalry.

Eastland adopted a different progressive life. Most animals on the Globe refused even to call it progressive; they called it Maoist after its inventor's name. It was secretive, repressive, and authoritarian. It required disciplined leaders who controlled and transformed the lives of the animals in Eastland into a life of methodical control based on the merits of hard work. The more you worked for the system, the more generous it was to you. Despite its questionable nature, Eastland's animals found it beneficial and adopted it with little resistance to the Chiefs.

The system required a continual supply of energy for the animals. Every animal on the Animal Globe required three rations of feed per day. Eastland's Chiefs, aware of the need for better time management to match and compete with Newfarm, decided that their animals could live on only two rations. They ordered their leading geese to find a food formula that could give Eastland's animals the needed body energy, in only two rations a day. The geese worked secretly for years to find a formula.

Then, one day in early winter, Mr. Goose found out that an animal's body could absorb food nutrients quicker if they consumed it wet rather than dry. The rest of the animals on the Globe ate their rations dried. His research concluded that the rate of nutrient absorption was quick enough that animals consuming the wet feed needed two rations only a day. Mr. Goose had to examine many animals' manure until he got the right wet formula of wheat, barley, water, apples, honey, and other secret ingredients. He did not know that a few formulas he had prepared were becoming poisonous.

After a few days, he had a fever. He took some rest, going back to his barn with his partner and chicks. His family took care of him. Besides the fever, he developed shortness of breath, both of which grew worse every day. After a few days, his partner and chicks developed a fever. Their neighbors, goats, sheep, hens, cattle, and pigs, took turns taking care of the chicks. Then, the entire family, one after the other, developed shortness of breath. The neighbors developed a fever and then shortness of breath. After two weeks, the entire neighborhood got sick. Mr. Goose died, and after him, so did his partner and two of his chicks.

The news alarmed Eastland's Chief Bulls. But they were more afraid of losing their influence and connections with other ranches and their leadership race with Newfarm. They kept the news of the developing disease a secret. But when neighboring ranch animals showed sickness symptoms, they had no choice but to confess.

The Chief of Chiefs said, "Some animals are getting sick, and we believe it is contagious. It spreads when animals touch each other! If animals want to survive, they must keep a safe distance from each other!"

However, the announcement came too late since penguins, goats, sheep, pigs, and hens visited Eastland and carried the disease to their ranches without their knowledge. They only developed sickness symptoms days after their return.

First, Rofield's animals got sick. Pigeons passed the slogan "save your life, keep your distance" to Rofield's animals, but they took it too lightly, and many of them got sick and died. It took pigeons much effort to relay the situation's seriousness to the Chief Bulls. Chief Bulls adopted different mechanisms to save animal life. There were too many variables to consider, the feed preparation, the honey production and consumption, planting, and harvesting, besides storehouse management. In a matter of days, the disease spread everywhere. Animal species were getting sick and were dying every minute of the day.

Expert geese within every ranch on the Globe designed their own plans of action. They referred to the plan as "animal-distancing." Animals having to do activities kept six feet from every adjacent animal. Many activities, such as planting and harvesting, store housing, and transportation of feed, depended on animals working near each other. As a result, many animals resisted the whole idea.

They said, "We need to feed our children; if we do not work, animals will die from hunger, not from the disease."

Other animals said, "You cannot decide for us what we should do; this is our freedom and our choice!"

More animals got sick and died on more ranches. After Rofield, Rhonefield was next, then Streamforest, Rhinefield, and the rest of Eurainia, the Midlands, Oceania, Australinea,

Newfarm, and everywhere.

When the Chief Bulls of these ranches knew their animals were not following animal-distancing, they had to intervene.

The Chiefs said, "We are going to impose animal-distancing using force if we must!"

They deployed their army of dogs to impose what they called a lockdown, which meant staying home.

They ordered, "Every animal must stay in his or her barn; every animal has to stay in their cubicle; no animal can go out!"

There was panic on these ranches. Animals thought the lockdown would starve them to death. They became even more defiant and ran out to get their feed rations. There were lines everywhere.

Things got out of control in many ranches. Animals were fighting each other for an extra ration. Then, the Chief Bull of each ranch announced that each animal would get his feed ration as scheduled but cautioned, "We must do it in an orderly manner."

They wrote this slogan everywhere, "No animal is going to starve; we will take care of you!"

Then, things calmed, and the rule of animal-distancing worked slowly but surely. Every ranch had a different pace of planning and implementation. In the meantime, more ranches got sick, and the disease reached Newfarm and Redfarm. In less than a month, the whole Globe became infected and affected.

Geese and other animals who spent most of their lives studying the science of healing animals continued researching, trying to understand why this disease happened and how it spread so expeditiously from one animal to another. They worked wholeheartedly. They tried to take as many precautions as possible against infection while they treated other animals. But the disease was so contagious that many got sick or died until they mastered the precautions against infection.

Chief Bulls from one ranch held meetings with Chief Bulls from other ranches. They held daily meetings with expert animals; they hoped that somebody could give them answers and solutions. But there were no magic solutions. The count of infected and dead animals on every ranch increased. Experts from the Animal Globe developed a graph from those numbers that helped them understand the disease's spread. They concluded that every ranch had to contend with a peak number of dead and infected animals. If they kept an intense animal-distancing procedure and kept most animals locked in their stalls, cubicles, and barns, they could flatten the curve. Then the number could decline. Chiefs, therefore, enforced a stricter lockdown.

In the meantime, animal life could not continue as before. Animals remained locked in their cubicles and barns. There was no more planting or harvesting for most of the animals unless their Chief Bulls allowed it. No more activities outside their barns, no more visits to each other. Ordinary animal life came to a halt.

CHAPTER EIGHTEEN

THE OLIVE TREE ENCOUNTER

The skies over the Meadow of the Olive Tree dimmed. Thunder and lightning accompanied a halo of bright light overshadowing the Olive Tree. A beam of light came from the center of the tree's massive trunk and percolated its three branches until they were glowing. The beams of lights extended through the tiny branches until they reached the nests of the Four Majesties, each of which was adorned with the wing color of the Majesty that nested on it. The Five Birds received a spell of electrifying presence. Black Rainbow flew from one Majesty to the other and then returned to his place.

Seminoles and penguin-Penguinists locked in their barns near the Meadow, who monitored the continued slow withering of the Olive Tree, could not believe themselves. For years, they only saw it wither. Pigeons and hawks circulated the news to the Animal Globe. Animals locked in their barns and ranches could not visit the Olive Tree because of the disease.

"What is going on with it?" they asked.

The nearby animals could see that there were beams of glowing light shining in the Five Majestic nests. Most of the time, Black Rainbow's nest glowed more, but sometimes, one or all of the Four Majesties' nests glowed simultaneously. They could hear the Majesties making noises, unlike the purrs or painful shrieks that they often heard from them. Animals could not figure out what was happening on the Tree. It looked to them that the Five Majestic Birds were having a conversation.

"Look at them, my daughters!" said Black Rainbow to the Majestic Four. "Look at them, locked in their small barns and cubicles, their hearts and minds full of fear from an unknown and unseen enemy. Already one species is blaming the other for causing the disease. One ranch is calling out another for causing it; they never learn, my daughters. What a shame. Animals never learn!"

The Four Majesties answered in one voice: "No, father, they never learn that they caused it!"

"Yes, they are all responsible for creating it. From the beginning, I gave animals a gift, the gift of life; I gave it to them for free. I created it with a delicate balance, and all I asked them to do was to keep and preserve it..."

Black Rainbow paused and turned to the animals witnessing the event.

"Animals have lost their purpose; animals have lost contact with their surroundings and the things that matter. Throughout their history, they insisted on cutting the breath of life from other animals. Perhaps this time, they will learn what it means when their own breath runs out or they experience the pain of an animal dear to them as he runs out of breath. Perhaps in the silence of their barns, they will reach out to the depths of their hearts and rediscover their real purpose."

Black Majesty asked, "What is the purpose of animals?"

Black Rainbow answered, "Their purpose is to preserve life by maintaining my balance."

Then, White Majesty said, "But some animals believe they are preserving the balance of life on the globe for future animal generations. They believe there are too many animals on the globe and the less fortunate must die; so, they let them die. They take their time before they react to droughts, WARs, starvation, and massacres."

"To those animals, I say, 'I created animals equal. Who has given you the authority to take my place? I created life, and I

preserve the right balance to sustain it. That is not your decision to make. Your role is to love one another by helping each other to live and not to die. Leave the rest to me!'"

The Four Majestic Birds said together, "But many animals do not believe that you even exist! They think they have to take matters into their own hands."

"To those who say that I do not exist, I say, 'You cannot see this invisible enemy. And yet, you witness his destructive actions. You believe he exists. You have locked down and stopped your life activities to protect yourselves. How is it possible that you see the marvelous, meticulously created wonders of the globe that you enjoy every day and cannot see my existence in it? Every creation needs a designer. Alternatives to my existence fall short of explaining how everything began and what still holds it together. How can the logic of chaos or the logic of randomness create so much order?'"

"But some animals say they love you, and they have many books, practices, and cults to prove that," said Green Majesty.

"I am HOLY and perfect. My doctrine is Love. My love is patient; my love is kind. It does not envy, it does not boast, it is not proud. It does not dishonor others, it is not self-seeking, it is not easily angered, it keeps no record of wrongs. Love does not delight in evil but rejoices with the truth. It always protects, always trusts, always hopes, always perseveres.

"Tell me, daughters, where is my love in the droughts, the WARs, and the atrocities they have created? They distorted my image and the meaning of my love. I love my creation; I love all animals. Any animal who claims to love me and does not love his neighbor, regardless of species and skin color, is not of me. He is lying to himself and me!"

"What do you mean?" they asked in chorus.

"I do not need cults that are void of my holy nature or void of the purpose of my creation. I created you Four to remind them of their purpose and the balance of life. How many times have I sent you, and they chose to disregard you! They even tried to get rid of you! Many animals consider you and even me their enemy! They want to get rid of us."

Red Majesty asked, "Will you let animals get rid of us?"

"You and I are one. Animals can choose to live with me or without me. Animals always have their free will. But they have to be responsible and accountable for their choices and actions."

"Does that mean that you will abandon them?" asked White and Red Majesties together.

"I never abandon my children. I have an infinite love for them. My time is infinite. They cannot see what I see, no matter how hard they try. I am the beginning and the end. Therefore, I can see the beginning and the end, both at the same time. What they see as evil today, I look at as an opportunity. They have disrupted and continue disrupting the balance of my creation —a balance that I created and crafted with meticulous care and precision. They have disturbed it by the droughts they caused, the habitat exploitation, the pollution of the air and the globe's atmosphere, and the WARs—they are masters. I am always willing to make out of every evil they create, even an invisible enemy, another means towards the preservation of life."

"How can life be preserved when there is so much death?" asked White Majesty.

"Many animals spend their lives trying to gain power and wealth, sometimes by killing each other. Now, they are using their power and wealth to save lives from more deaths. Many animals are busy gathering wealth and power, forgetting their family and friends' existence, who end up living a lonely life wishing they were never born!"

Black Majesty asked, "But if they learned little over thousands of years, do you think it will work this time?"

"The pace of development and freedoms animals gained have been on a constant increase. Look what they did with it! Animals have separated themselves from my love and think that using their minds alone is enough for them to be masters of their destiny. They have lost contact with their inner self for a long time. They forgot that their destiny is contingent on having a balanced relationship between mind, soul, and heart with me. They adopted a life system that leaves no time to sit with themselves and think about life's questions and purpose. I so much want them to grow up; this last halt to every aspect of their life can take them on a voyage within their souls. Now, this unseen enemy has stripped them equally. He does not care about their wealth or riches, characters, or egos. Animals are now equal! Their consciousness, minds, and hearts are now focused on one thing: survival."

The Four Majesties asked in one voice, "What is the lesson you want them to learn this time?"

"My lesson has always been and will always be the same, ***to preserve life by preserving the balance***"

The Four Majesties resumed asking in one voice, "Can you elaborate, father? What does that mean from your point of view? Because they don't understand."

"Some animals refuse to accept my existence. Others accept my existence but misconceive my nature. Still others have a good grasp of my nature, yet that blessing is their curse. They do not know how to live in the dynamics of a fraudulent system. Often, you find these animals using self-isolation as a tool to preserve themselves from being hurt or because they are afraid of the challenge. They leave animals without guidance, who become more susceptible to the teachings of predators or hunters. Often, even when they engage, they may not assume a role that can enhance a positive change towards animals' real purpose on the globe: to preserve the balance. In these three cases, animals usually adopt life mechanisms that disrupt the purposes of their creation, my creation, and the cycle of innovative violence continues.

"Daughters, I base my creation on an intricate system of connections and interconnections, both external and internal, encompassing animals' relationship to the globe and animals' relationships with each other. A disruption to the outer atmosphere, for example, will have effects on the inner atmosphere, then the oceans, then the land, and will ultimately affect animal life.

"In their relations with each other, animals have disrupted the balance of my creation by adopting many systems based on their misconceptions of my nature. From the moment of creation, I created you, daughters,"

Black Rainbow paused, looked up to the skies and then back at the four White Majesties with an affectionate embracing smile.

"I created you and kept sending you to remind them of my love and that it was their responsibility to preserve it. You, Lady Truth, Lady Mercy, Lady Justice, and Lady Peace, are the tools of the shining presence of my love. Whenever the four of you are present together, purring with satisfaction, you generate Hope.

"Yes, my daughters, Hope is the rational and superior product of encounters with you. Hope is the most crucial ingredient for animal salvation. Hope based on your presence is the only way to combat hate, greed, ego, lust, pain, and power.

"Since creation, and throughout history, any action animals took in which you, my daughters, were not present in a balanced manner led to droughts and WARs, to atrocities and suffering. Such actions of animals were akin to animals who built their barns on the sand. When the winds and the floods came, they took their barns away.

"But, when animals built their barns on solid rock and enacted proper balance of my Four Lady Majesties, there were prolonged times of harmony, respect, and coexistence. No matter how strong the winds and the floods were, their barns survived.

"Now, my daughters, how many times have I sent each of you to warn animals about their actions? How many times did they reject you and they went on with their attitudes? Most animals still cannot comprehend that I am right there with them; I feel everything they feel! I feel everything you feel!"

Just then, the animals noticed what appeared to be light beams flowing from each Majesty to the others and then into Black Rainbow. The rays' speed increased until Black Rainbow's body absorbed them. The color of his body turned almost red. Black Rainbow anguished and shed a tear with every ray he received. Upon receiving the last beam, he cried out with massive pain, and a stream of tears flowed from his eyes through the trunk of the Tree, as if watering the flowers.

The Majestic Four, with tears in their eyes, said in one voice, "Their eyes are blurred; they don't see how much you love them!"

Every tear the Four Ladies shed was a recollection of a tragedy committed by animals throughout history. They remembered them with such intensity that Black Rainbow felt it too and broke into tears himself.

The animals soon saw that everything had returned to its previous radiant look. The Five Majesties resumed what appeared to be a conversation.

"Will you ever forgive them, father?" asked Black Majesty.

"What father would I be if I did not follow my own rules? I am the living image and fulfillment of each one of you, daughters. I can forgive them if they ask me in honesty," answered Black Rainbow.

They asked in one voice, "As a loving father, what do you want to tell your children?"

"I miss all my children; I miss their voices talking to me!

"To those who say that they know me and love me, I say, 'You cannot love me while adhering to an incomplete understanding of my nature.' I ask them, 'How can you be fair and good when you hide behind a wall of fear, anger, and selfish desires that criticize, stereotype, blame, and judge and cause bigotry and hatred, sometimes even in my name?' If you know me, then you know what I stand for, and I am always consistent. I never change my mind on issues of truth, mercy, justice, and peace.

I tell them, 'Be fair and consistent as I am fair and consistent. There is room for every animal at the convocation of victory.'

"To those who say I do not exist yet have high moral codes, I ask, 'If I do not exist, where are your morality and conscience coming from? How do you know the difference between good and evil? You try to be good and fair. But how can you be fair and good when you hide behind a wall of fear, anger, and selfish desires that criticize, stereotype, blame, and judge and cause bigotry and hatred? You need to work on truth, mercy, justice, and peace. Be fair and consistent. There is room for every animal at the convocation of victory.'

"To those who do not know me and have no moral codes, I say, 'The choices you make today have repercussions for another day. Beware! There is plenty of room at the convocation of the wicked!'

"And to every animal species on the Animal Globe, I say, 'You have created a system that is supposed to promote animal rights, animal dignity, and animal equality. Endorse it to its fullest and keep your eyes on the prize: Hope. Where there is hope, there is reconciliation.

"'Think globally, act locally, and keep the four elements of Truth, Mercy, Justice, and Peace at the core of every decision.'

"'In everything, do to others as you would have them do to you!'

"'Do not create cults, but create hope.'

"Then, you will preserve life and restore the balance of creation!

"Leave the rest to me!"

And the Five Majesties said in one voice, *"For animal life to continue, life has to be preserved and the balance restored."*

The animals watching the mysterious event at the Meadow of the Olive Tree observed the skies clearing, the cloud disappearing, and the rays of glowing light dimming. Each one of the Five Majesties assumed their usual positions and colors. And the Olive Tree returned to its withering condition.

———————— ❖ ————————

The next day, Black Rainbow sent out White Majesty, Lady Justice, to one of Newfarm's Terrains, where a hate crime was in progress. Newfarm was the most progressive ranch on the Animal Globe. White Majesty identified four dogs arguing with a black Angora goat named Floyd. They thought Floyd broke the rules of Newfarm's Chief Bulls. Many animals were watching the developing incident. Floyd tried to explain his innocence.

Lady Justice flew in circles in the sky above the dogs, crying and shrieking with agony as if someone were torturing her. She shed her white feathers everywhere. The four dogs saw her but disregarded her. They forced Floyd, who caused no threat to their lives, to the ground as two of them sat on him. One of them, having a look of gratification at what he was doing, thrust the weight of his entire body onto Floyd's neck. Lady Justice shed her wet feathers on the dog's head, but the dog did not care. Animals present tried to tell him that Floyd couldn't breathe, but he kept a calm demeanor, showing no signs of compassion.

Floyd, in a frail voice that kept fading with every second, kept pleading, "I can't breathe!"

The dog, unconcerned, kept pushing on his neck for a few minutes until Floyd died.

The animals present shared the information about Floyd's unwarranted murder with other animals on the ranch. Many animals were angered at dogs who used excessive brutality while enforcing ranch rules against black Angora goats for no other reason than the goats' color. Fearing that this unwarranted dog behavior would go unpunished as it did in many similar cases in the past, Angora goats left their barns and cubicles. They headed to their Terrains centers to demand justice for Floyd and animals with similar but untold stories.

In no time, thousands of animals of many species living in Newfarm started protests…, and the demonstrations continued for days. Pigeons carried the message and reached the four corners of the Animal Globe. Thousands of animals on many ranches facing similar cases joined the demonstrations in their respective ranches.

When Lady Justice returned to her nest, Black Rainbow sent Green Majesty, Lady Peace, to Yemini. He sent Black Majesty, Lady Truth, to Applefield, and Red Majesty, Lady Mercy, to central Olympia when she returned.

Black Rainbow, the loving father, continued sending them day after day, hour after hour.

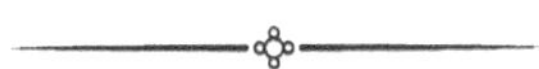

Then, one day, on a cold winter morning, Chiefs were simultaneously sitting in their barns of their respective ranches reflecting on the life of animals. They were contemplating the case of Floyd, an innocent Angora goat killed in Newfarm by vicious dogs because of an unfair and corrupt system of checks and balances; a global disease that had brought the life of animals to a halt; a severe disturbance to the Animal Globe's atmosphere that had catastrophic effects on animal life; and a raging, endless conflict at the Meadow of the Olive Tree.

Each Chief was independently, yet simultaneously experiencing the same event. He was so caught in deep thought that he did not notice a pigeon standing on the porch near his window calling his name. The pigeon called and knocked with his beak on the glass window near the Chief's stall.

"Chief, Chief." said the pigeon.

Finally, the Chief noticed him. He sprang up, opened the window, and let him in.

"Oh, I am sorry, pigeon, I was deep in thought and hardly noticed you," he said with a cautious smile.

"Well, I have sad news for you. The whole Globe is imposing new rules that confine animals," said the pigeon. "All over the Animal Globe, the number of animals allowed to work has been diminished. Animals can barely work, and they are finding it hard to feed their little ones."

Alarmed and disappointed, the Chief said, "I am not surprised; it was only a matter of time for this to happen."

The pigeon asked, "What do you want to do, Chief?"

Saddened by the news, the Chief looked puzzled. The pigeon watched and thought he detected tears in his eyes when he said, "Animals do not deserve this treatment; they have been treated unjustly and have been misled for too long. The animals have to live to their full potential, have a decent life and a hopeful pursuit of happiness."

At this moment, the Chief turned away from the pigeon. He looked distant, as if in a different world. The Chief cried out, "What is wrong with the Animal Globe? What can I do to restore animal life?" His agonizing tone became even higher. "Tell the Chiefs on the Globe that I want to meet them soon."

The pigeon flew to the four corners of the Globe; in no time, the Chiefs convened a meeting.

The issue at hand concerned not only the future of one ranch but every ranch, every animal, on the Animal Globe...

Final Word

For it is not true that the work of man is finished,
That we have nothing more to do in the world,
That we are just parasites in this world,
That it is enough for us to walk in step with the world,
For the work of man is only just beginning
and it remains to conquer all,
The violence entrenched in the recess of his passion,
And no race holds a monopoly of beauty,
of intelligence, of strength,
and,

There is a place for all at the Rendezvous of Victory.

Aimé Césaire

Animal Globe is a story about free will.
Every animal has a choice…!?

And every choice has a consequence.

Mercy and truth are met together;
righteousness and peace have kissed each other.

(Psalm 85:10 KJV)

Acknowledgments

Writing this novel took many years before reaching its final version. I am grateful to my teacher and good friend, Maxwell Miller, who was one of the first to read the original draft and provided valuable input. I would like to thank Dr. Peter Makari for his continued support, comments, and proofreads. A special acknowledgment to Prof. Ilan Pappe, author and historian, for reading the original and the final manuscripts, providing comments, advice, and the forward to the novel. But, nobody deserves more credit and appreciation than my wife, Caroline, whose love and support have been the inspiration and driving force behind this novel. I will always be indebted to you for allowing me to discover the author in me.

My thanks and appreciation go to a long list of friends and volunteers who helped read the manuscript over various stages of its writing and gave valuable input and advice. The list includes Terry Boron, Fran Acquarulo, Ellen Quagliaroli, Regis O'Neil, Kenneth Gorman, Charles Jackowski, Dorothee R. Caulfield, Dr. Linda Rammler, Greg Jansen, Bev Mello, Mary Walsh, Karen Whiting, and especially author Anne Gormley.

From Jerusalem, I want to thank Nora Kort for her comments on the first draft. Also, Usama Emerezian, his family, and staff at Emerezian Printing and Publishing for designing the book and its cover.

I want to thank the Sabella family, my mother Esperance, and my brothers and sisters, the Rock family, for their continued encouragement.

A special appreciation to Tony Sabella for his contribution in the editing of the manuscript. A similar appreciation goes to Andrew Stump for his detailed and extensive final proofread.

I am almost sure that I have missed a few people who have provided support, encouragement, and ideas over a drink or a conversation. Some might have also read the manuscript, and I have failed to mention their names. To you all, please consider this a personal thank you.